With All of Me

Book One:

Giuliana

By Joanne Fisher

Acknowledgements

Published in the United States of America, in the year 2024, by Joanne's Books, LLC. www.joannesbooks.com

Book Cover by: Macred Designs

https://www.robin-mcdonald.com/home.html

Edited by Daniel B. Fisher

ISBN: 9798883929402

DEDICATION

Dedicated to my wonderful husband, Danny.

You are not only a husband to me; you are my mentor, my editor, my bodyguard, my legal advisor, my lover, my soulmate and most importantly, my true companion. I have loved you since 2002 and I will love you until God calls me home.

WITH ALL OF ME

BOOK ONE

CHAPTER ONE

October 2005

She stood there, staring through the Intensive Care Unit window at him. He was lying on that hospital bed with all those wires and machines attached to his arms, chest and head. As tears streaked down her cheeks, she felt so guilty. It was her fault that he had almost died. A heart attack! While he was making love to her!

They were celebrating her birthday on that special weekend. They had gone to dinner in a fancy downtown Toronto restaurant and then headed for the hotel room that he had booked for them. They couldn't meet very often so they took advantage of all the opportunities they could get, seeing how they both were so busy. She was a manager at NCR, a company that produced medical devices used for Cancer Research. He was the Vice President of B & B Pharmaceuticals. Between business meetings, business trips that took him and her halfway around the world, and time dedicated to their respective families, she took the leftovers. Leftovers of small shreds of time. They had become very rare occasions when they could both get away from their respective families and spend a few peaceful and romantic hours together. She had always felt she was stealing his time and he had always assured her that it wasn't true. He cherished his time spent with Giuliana.

She covered her face with her hands as she was thinking of that tragic moment. She was on top of him, mounting him. Her eyes were closed as he pushed upward to give her that gift of ecstasy and pleasure while he had his hands tightly around her hips guiding her up and down. Suddenly, she didn't feel him anymore. She dismounted and turned on the light. His hands were clutching his chest, and his eyes were rolling backwards. She was terrified.

"Aaron! Aaron!" She cried as she slapped his face a few

times; "Oh my God! Oh my God! No…No…don't die…here…no…no!" She desperately cried as she kissed him all over his face.

He had always enjoyed every minute spent with her. She was able to relieve him of the heavy weight of stress and constant worries he had been withstanding throughout all these years, even if it was for a few hours. He had never regretted that first date. He could still remember when he saw her the first time. Even if he was very skeptical about it, he knew it was truly love at first sight.

Giuliana was a very patient woman. Right from the start, she understood his situation and she was happy to get whatever she could of him because she loved him. She knew from the start that his career came before everything, even his family. She was third in line, and she knew that's the way it was supposed to be, for Aaron. She fell in love with him from that very first night they met. She never admitted to herself that she could fall for a man she met on chat, but she did. Giuliana heard many internet love stories, some with positive endings and some negative. Some were horror stories. At that time, she felt it was a very safe, fresh and new way to discreetly meet a man or a woman.

She thought she saw a vague smile on his face. Was he thinking about her? He did look peaceful though, like he was resting. She knew he needed to rest, and she had always made it clear to him, from day one. Thank God, he was out of danger and that was most important for her right now. She placed her right hand on the glass and noticed the ring Aaron gave her. She wore it only in his presence, because it symbolized the love that united them. Tears rolled down her face when she realized that their relationship was over. That didn't matter right now. What mattered now was that he was alive and that he was given another chance. It was up to him now to realize what kind of life he was living and the consequences that came from that lifestyle. Even his wife would scold him from time to time about his lifestyle and she always agreed with his wife on that.

His wife...there she stood...also staring at him through the other window. She was surrounded by her family. The two

4

sons he always boasted about, the youngest son's wife and the granddaughter he loved so much but rarely found the time to be a grandfather too. She had never met his wife, or seen her, for that matter. The only thing she knew about her physical aspect was that she had lost weight following some diet. Giuliana could relate to that because she also had lost weight, but only following a strict diet given to her from her family doctor. She noticed that he wasn't as dark as her; he looked more Mediterranean than East Asian. Her first impression was that his wife was a classic, humble, patient, tried, East Asian, Catholic woman.

His wife noticed that she was staring at her. Although she was very thankful to her for saving his life, she couldn't help but be angry and jealous of her as well. She looked Mediterranean and certainly not over 40. She could never compete with her. God, look at her, she was a beautiful, mature, full bodied woman with full breasts, luscious lips, big brown eyes and, most of all, fair, olive skin. She was certain that out of all her physical features, it was her fair skin that had attracted him to that woman. She hated her but she had to maintain her calm for her children.

She was Sri-Lankan-born and raised with very dark skin like every Sri-Lankan. He was half Irish and half Sri-Lankan and therefore had lighter skin that other people she grew up with, which made him very popular with the local girls.

Patrick Gallagher was totally against his son marrying a Sri-Lankan girl. He wanted his son to marry a fair-skinned Irish girl. It was enough that he had married one. He didn't want the same destiny for his son, Aaron. At that time, he was 19 and he was studying. Patrick had decided that when he had his degree, he would take his son to Ireland for a graduation gift. Hopefully, he would meet a pretty Irish girl, marry her, and live there for the rest of his life.

Aaron was about to start his first year of university when he met this young Sri-Lankan girl, who was also attending the same school. They began to see each other occasionally without compromising their studies. Vivian had fallen for him almost immediately and found herself not being able to say no to him. The situation became serious when she got pregnant. To his father's disappointment, he had no choice but to marry her. That was it, you get a girl into trouble and once you're married, it's sacred, that's what Catholic Irish believed, therefore no objection. Seven months later his first son was born. He had to finish university so his father, Aaron Gallagher Senior, took them into his home and they lived together until Aaron got his degree. She knew that her father-in-law had always despised her, and he never forgave her for getting herself pregnant by his precious Aaron. Aaron was very well aware of the intentions of his father for his favorite and only son. He knew he had disappointed his father, so he decided to never argue with him in any way. He was grateful to his father. He could have very well kicked him out with his Sri-Lankan wife and son, but he didn't. As an old-fashioned Irish Catholic, he didn't.

As soon as Aaron finished school, he accepted a position in Holland where he began a new life with his own family. Two years later his second son was born, and he had totally dedicated his life to his work, children and wife. There were many occasions to have an affair in Holland. So many fair skinned women, you could take your pick. They were all gorgeous, tall, blonde haired, blue eyed, fair skinned women but he became so ambitious that he didn't want to spoil it with a Dutch lover.

As the years went by, Aaron got tired of his sex life with Vivian. Her love making was boring and Aaron had other needs and sexual fantasies that she would never consent to. Therefore, around the ten-year mark of their marriage, Aaron decided it was time to see who he was out there and maybe could find himself an open minded, northern European woman. He would also prefer her to be married so he wouldn't have to commit to her. He couldn't permit himself to lose his family now; it was too precious to him. His career was going well enough that he could permit himself to have an affair on the side.

In the early 2000s, a colleague told him that there was a new and safe way to meet women. There was a possibility to pick and choose who you wanted to meet. It was called online chat and Aaron gave it a try. He became immediately hooked! He began chatting with many women, all married and all available. There was one woman in particular that attracted his attention. She was from Germany and her name was Gilda. From her photograph he could see that she was very unhappy and unsatisfied with her marriage. He also noted how beautiful and sensual she was. They immediately hit it off on chat, then they began exchanging emails, then the phone calls started, then the sexual encounters began. At that point, they fell in love with each other, but they mutually decided to see each other whenever they could but without commitment. The affair had lasted until Aaron was transferred to Canada. They managed to spend one week together in Vienna and never saw each other again.

She knew this was going on for a while now. Just like she also knew about the woman he had when they were living in Holland. A wife always knows. All those business dinners with important clients and trips to the casino because he knew she hated gambling. How many times he came home smelling of her perfume. She could smell it as she was lying in bed faking to be asleep while he took off his clothes and laid them on the chair. She would get up and smell them as he was taking a quick shower and ran like a thief into bed again when he was done. He hadn't touched her for such a long time, and she couldn't remember the last time they had sex. But as a good, traditional Sri-Lankan wife, she never said a word to him. She kept it all inside her. He had become very important and ambitious man. She wouldn't dare ruin his reputation by leaving or divorcing him although she had tried to stop him at one point but without success. He resumed his affair a few months later and she gave up. She couldn't pretend to always have him to herself; she never did and never will.

Vivian did try to stop him once, but she failed miserably. He stopped for a couple of months but once again, he became bored with dedicating his life to his family and he went back for more. At that point, Vivian had no more power.

Damn it! She did have her pride. She had to fight for him and for her family. Although he had many chances, he never left her or his family. He belonged to her and to his family. Who was she kidding? They were married, yes, but he was never hers. She knew very well who he belonged to now. Well, if he came out of this medical problem, then she would make sure he never went back to that woman again. She had a plan this time.

She did have her children, and her grandchildren. Aaron didn't know that another grandchild was on the way. They were organizing a surprise party to announce it next month, so they could tell the entire family. She also had her beautiful home that she decorated all by herself. She saved her husband a boat load of money on home decorators, and he seemed to have appreciated that. Aaron figured that she would have been happy with all the material things he provided for her. Lately, though, she was feeling that emptiness in her life. An emptiness that wasn't there in the first years of their marriage but over the years it slowly made its presence between them.

CHAPTER TWO

Giuliana was wondering what his wife was thinking.

"She probably hates my guts." She thought to herself.

She felt sorry for her. She was the other woman! Did she want to tear her eyes out or did she want to thank her for being where she was when he had the attack. God, she was so curious…and ashamed…and sorry. Giuliana turned to look at him again. She loved Aaron so much. She almost died herself when he was lying in bed, unconscious. She immediately called reception screaming:

"Send an ambulance! Hurry, Hurry! Oh my God! He's dying! Hurry!"

She was still naked when the paramedics pounded on the door. She grabbed the bed spread and wrapped it around herself just as she opened it to let them in. The paramedics flew in. They immediately gave him oxygen and began revitalizing him. After a few interminable minutes, they got his heart beating again and conscious. She grabbed his hand as he weakly smiled at her.

"I love you, Aaron! You'll be okay. I promise!"

And she kissed him lightly on the lips. When they were gone with him, she plunged to the floor and cried. She was still shaking but she was relieved. She knew he was going to be fine now. He was in good hands. She slowly got dressed and went to the hospital.

Vivian noticed her youngest son was staring at that woman. He let go of his mother's hands and began to walk towards her. She was staring at Aaron and didn't notice him coming closer. He cleared his throat and she turned to look at him.

"Giuliana?" he asked.

"Oh, you know who I am?" she asked.

"Oh yes. I checked my father's phone and I saw the text messages and I put 2 and 2 together." he clarified.

He spoke to her softly as he put his hand on her arm. She had tears running down her cheeks.

"I'm so sorry! I really don't know what else to say

except that I'm sorry."

"I'm a man and I know my father very well. I'm here to thank you. If he wasn't with you, he probably would have died. You saved his life so thank you."

Vivian could see them from where she was standing. Then she put her hand on his shoulder, said something to him, turned to look at Aaron and walked away. Terry walked back towards his mother and brother Patrick.

"What did you say to her?" She asked.

"I just thanked her…for being there…and for saving his life. I know you don't want to hear this, Mom, but if it weren't for her, Dad would be dead." He turned to look at his father.

"You're right. I don't want to hear it! But I have to admit it. But this is so embarrassing! How can we face our family and friends or his business partners?" She covered her face with her hands.

"Mom, there's nothing to face! She's gone! We're here, right? He had the attack at home, that's all. She understands the situation perfectly. She knows what position he's in. She promised me that. Don't worry, okay?"

"What did you say to her exactly?"

"I simply thanked her and kindly asked her to leave. She said she understood completely and that she wouldn't do anything to hurt him because..." He stumbled.

"Because?" his mother asked.

"She loves him."

Giuliana looked at Aaron one more time before she left. She wanted to make sure he was okay. She was afraid when she saw his son standing in front of her. Instead, he was very kind and understanding. What a sweet boy. No wonder Aaron was so proud of him. Terry did do what he was not able to ......marry a white woman and marry for love. His wife Meagan's skin was as white as snow with deep blue eyes and light blond hair. Terry's daughter was not as fair as her mother, but she had exotic beauty. A mixture of two worlds, Asia and America. Certainly, she would not have had any problems like her grandparents. Giuliana knew everything about Aaron's family. He had shown pictures of his Patrick and Terry with his wife and granddaughter on their first date.

He never showed her a picture of his wife, and she had always asked herself why. She had shown Aaron pictures of her family also on that first date. She took out the precious photos she had in her wallet. She had her whole family there. Her husband, her three children, her father, her sister, her sister's children, her mother and a photo of her when she was in high school. She still remembers his remarks about that photo.

"Wow, you don't look much older, but you sure look better!" He gave her that look. She blushed just as she did in the days that photo was taken.

"Thank you." She answered him.

Then she pulled out a photo of her and Aaron. It was taken in one of those photo booths that were found in shopping malls. She kept two of the photos and the other two were for Aaron. He had it tucked away in his wallet, and she did the same. She loved those photos. They both were the epitome of a hidden love that was greater than any love they had experienced. She looked at it intensely and gently slid it back

into   her   wallet.

CHAPTER THREE

As she was walking down the hallway, she noted the time. 2:15 am. Boy, she thought, it was late. Rocco was going to shoot her for sure this time. No, he wasn't clever enough to understand what was going on. All these years, he never suspected a thing. She had always told him half-truths. The usual night out with the girls at work or a night at the theatre, the movies, a quick drink after work. She also told him that many times their husbands came with them. He even knew about Aaron. He knew that he was one of the girl's husbands and that he came along once in a while. Giuliana always had good explanations on her whereabouts, and he had always believed her. He trusted her. He had always trusted her. She had decided a few years back that she had no intention of waiting for him to go out with her. She wanted to have fun.

"Life is short, Rocco, and I want to live it a little." He understood. As always.

Rocco loved to stay home. He didn't like the movies,

theatre or going drinking with his friends. He only had a few friends, and they were at the Italian bakery, where he went to on Sunday mornings when Giuliana went to church with the kids. He liked to garden and fix things up at home. They had a big house and there was always something to do. He also loved his job and enjoyed working. He never said no to overtime or to his boss. He had been working in construction for over twenty-three years now and he had no intention of losing it.

He also enjoyed bringing the kids here and there. His oldest, Samuele was in his second year of university. He was studying Science or his master's or something like that. He wasn't into his kids' school much, but he sure was proud of them. He was happy to bring his second son, Gabriele, wherever he wanted to go. He didn't have his driver's license yet, so he happily took him here and there. His daughter, Anastasia, was the light of his eyes. When she was born, he showed her to the whole ward while his wife was still under anesthesia from the C-section. She was a beautiful girl, just like her mother. The same eyes as her mother and the same rebel personality as her mother. She was straight A student and always helped around the house when her mother wasn't home. She was also a spoiled brat. Whatever Anastasia wanted; Anastasia got.

Rocco was a good man, a good father and a good husband. He had loved Giuliana from that very night he met her in that discotheque. He still loved her after 22 years of marriage. He remembered how the first few years of marriage were the hardest ones. She was not used to living on a farm, alone, in the middle of nowhere. She was a city girl, Torontonian born and raised. Even if she came from an Italian family, she was free to come and go as she pleased without overdoing it. Her father was strict but fair and she always got her way with him. He adored her and she never disrespected him. She always asked if she could go out with her friends or go to a party. He always knew where she was, and she was always waiting for him when it was time to be picked up and brought home.

Rocco was alone then, his father had just died, and his

mother had Alzheimer, she was kept in a nursing home. He was fixing up his parents' home to accommodate him and his new wife. (As soon as he found one.)

He had gone out that night with his friends as he usually did. They had decided to go to "Sayonara" on Yorkville Avenue that night instead of the usual place. They were looking around to see if there were any interesting girls. About an hour later he and his friends had spotted a pair of girls. They looked alike, probably sisters. They were gorgeous! One was thinner and taller than the other one. They began the usual argument about who was going after whom. There were fifteen of them and only two girls. They would let the girls decide. Giuliana and Caterina found themselves surrounded by guys. Wow, this had never happened to them. They could take their pick. One was just as good looking as the other. Giuliana noticed a very dark and handsome guy with a moustache. His shirt was open to his stomach to show off a manly, hairy chest and he had the most beautiful blue eyes. He had noticed that she was staring at him, so he asked her to dance.

"So, what's your name?" he asked.

"Giuliana and you?" Those eyes!

"Peter, nice to meet you." He wasn't looking at her eyes.

"Likewise." She blushed.

They danced a couple of dances then the rest of the group joined in. She noticed that another one of his friends was dancing very close to her. He was trying to get a closer look at her. He was just as tall as her and not as good looking as Peter. She noticed that he was shyer than Peter. But Peter was really something to look at.

"Can you tell me your name?" He asked.

"Giuliana. What's yours?" Not that she cared much.

"Frank. You know, you're very beautiful." He just couldn't get enough of looking at her.

"Thanks." She blushed again. He was beginning to interest her. "What do you do Frank?"

"I'm a truck driver." He looked at the floor when he said that.

"Interesting." Not really.

"Would you go out with me tomorrow? You know, it's my birthday and I would love to spend it with you. I'll come pick you up at 7." He was quick.

"Oh, I don't know......my dad...."

"Don't worry about your dad, we can meet somewhere. Make up an excuse, please." He sounded so desperate.

"Okay, why not." Too quick. She was intrigued.

"Fantastic!" His face lit up.

They danced together for a while then Giuliana went to spend some time with a few guys she knew. He followed her the rest of the night and never took his eyes off her. She was also keeping an eye on him too.

On their way home, Giuliana kept telling Caterina how much she liked Frank.

"He's not that great looking but he said I was beautiful; do you believe it? ME, beautiful. I've never been called beautiful by anyone in my entire life. I've always been the fat one and..."

"Giuliana, stop putting yourself down. Yes, I know you've always been fatter than me, but your face seems made of porcelain and mine is full of acne. So, there you go, we're even!" She seemed irritated when Giuliana always put herself down. She had to stop it.

"Ok, fine. You're right, you're always right. You've always been the smarter one too. You've got your head screwed on the right way, not like me. You see, I meet a guy and already I'm going on and on about him."

"You must be falling for him already." Caterina could see that in her sister's eyes.

"No way! I just met him! Yes, I do like him, but it's not love." She didn't look in her sister's eyes as she said that.

"No, eh? Ok, sis, whatever you say!" she said as she chuckled to herself.

The next night, Frank met Giuliana in front of an Italian Sport Bar on St. Clair Street. They had a cappuccino and a couple of Italian pastries. They decided to stroll up and down Little Italy. Frank took Giuliana's hand, as he stopped, and he confessed to her that his name wasn't Frank but Rocco. He wasn't a truck driver either, he had a vineyard in St. Catherine's. He even pulled out his driver's license to show her he wasn't lying. He wanted to be totally honest with this girl because he really liked her a lot and he was sure she liked him too.

When Giuliana heard his confession, at first, she was angry, then she looked into his eyes and it was at that moment that she fell in love with him.

Eleven months later, they were married. Their wedding was Giuliana's dreams come true. She had always dreamed of having a wedding like hers. Rocco paid for almost everything because he had been saving his money for a few years now. Her mother, being a dressmaker, sewed her wedding dress. They picked out the furniture, together. They decorated their newly renovated home, together. It was great. She was in seventh heaven. She even lost weight, naturally, without dieting. She was just so busy, excited and happy; she didn't find time to eat.

Giuliana and Rocco went on their honeymoon in Italy, as many Italian Canadian couples do. They stayed in Italy for three weeks, visiting their relatives but also cities like Roma, Venice, Florence, Milan and Verona (the hometown of Romeo and Juliet). Giuliana was adamite about visiting Verona.

Almost two years later Samuele was born. He was very special to her because he was her first born and also because he looked just like his father. Also, because he was the first grandson, he was the pride and joy of Giuliana's parents.

Rocco continued working on his farm and Giuliana stayed home and raised Samuele. A few years later, they went on holiday to Florida for a couple of weeks in the summer. When they got home, Giuliana found out she was pregnant again. She told everyone on a Sunday afternoon, just as the family was sitting down for dinner.

"You know, Samuele, you're going to have a little brother or sister. Would you like that?" she said as she lifted her head to look at Rocco and smiled. He immediately went over to her and hugged her so hard; she almost couldn't breathe.

"Rocco, not so hard! You're squeezing two of us now." And she kissed him.

Seven months later Gabriele was born. He was a huge baby weighing over eleven pounds. He looked exactly like his mother and Rocco fell in love with him just as he did when he met his mother.

But his pride and joy was his beautiful Anastasia and when she arrived, he showed her off to the entire hospital ward. She had captured Daddy's heart the moment she came into this world.

When Anastasia was two years old, Giuliana and Rocco decided to sell the vineyard and to move to the suburbs. They had been living there for over fifteen years now and Giuliana was beginning to get restless. She was born in Toronto and wanted to go back there, but Rocco wasn't born in the big city, he was a country boy. Finally, they agreed to move to Oakville, a smaller city just outside of Toronto. They bought a beautiful, bigger home in a new subdivision and every child had their own room. Giuliana was very content now and that was all Rocco wanted was to see Giuliana happy.

Giuliana was thinking about the past twenty-two years

spent with Rocco as she drove home that night. They were the most wonderful years of her life and she still loved Rocco very much, but it was Aaron she wanted to spend the rest of her life with now, and not Rocco. Tears began to cloud Giuliana's eyes, so she stopped the car on the side and let all her desperation, guilt and anguish come out and fill the packet of tissues in her purse.

Then Marina popped into her mind. Marina was her confident and she was always there when Giuliana needed someone to talk to. She would have called her in the morning. She had made a final decision with her life and wanted Marina to know before anyone else.

CHAPTER FOUR

Three Years Earlier

Giuliana was surfing the net almost every day since she got laid off in August. She had begun chatting while she was searching for work. She loved chatting. She had met so many people, both men and women but her favorite chat buddies were men. She tried to keep her friends around her age. She disliked young people since she found they were arrogant and condescending. Well, most of them were.

Many of the men she chatted with had other intentions, but she was not interested in cyber-sex. She didn't believe that you could get pleasure out of something like that. She preferred the real thing. Sometimes she did get a little carried away because a few of her buddies were very good with words and claimed that they were able to go on for hours. A lot of times they were able to get her in the mood. All of these chat buddies were always begging her to go out with them. She never even considered it. It was out of the question. Even if she became very tempted at times but it was only Rocco she wanted. It was always Rocco she wanted. Then when she got into bed with Rocco, she would actually have the sex that all her cyber buddies begged her for online. She used to enjoy it but not lately. It was monotonous and rapid. Sometimes she wondered if those chat buddies were actually serious of the claims that they made to her online. Who knows…maybe one day she would find out.

In Spring, she finally landed a job as an Administrative Assistant at NCR, a company that produced medical devices used for Cancer Research. She would assist the international sales department and she was ecstatic that she had found such a wonderful company and with a magnificent cause. On top of that, the pay was very good.

Now that she was working again, she seldom went online. She was very choosy to whom she chatted with. Only the ones she was particularly intimate with. Some of them confided in her, they told her their secrets about their wives, girlfriends and so on. She was always of help to them because she portrayed a woman's point of view. She limited herself to only chatting with a couple of close online friends: one was Bobby from California and Charles from Australia. She rarely chatted with Charles because of the time difference but Bobby was always there for her, no matter the time.

One evening in May, she was checking her emails and to see if any of her buddies were online. She received a message.

'Hi there. Would you like to chat?'

She checked the information window. She always checked the person's information. Then she decided whether to accept the chat or not. She noticed this individual was a man in his fifties. He gave the message that he was a business professional and that he just wanted good, clean chat.

She accepted.

'Sure, why not.'

> *'Well, then, why don't you tell me your name?'*

'Giuliana and yours?'

> *'Aaron. Tell me Giuliana, are you married?'*

'Yes, for almost 19 years and you?'

> *'Not bad. Yes, I am. Longer than you. I have two sons and a granddaughter.'*

'Wow, you're a pretty young grandfather.'

> *'I know. I got married very young. Do you have kids, Giuliana?'*

'Yes, three. Two boys and a girl.'

> *'Busy woman.'*

'Yes, but I love them.'

*'Of course, you do. It's very natural.
Do you work, Giuliana.'*

*'Yes, I just started a job about a month ago. Customer Service
Representative. What do you do Aaron?'*

*'I'm a Vice President of a medium
sized pharmaceutical company.*

'Wow, a V.P. Not bad. You must be very busy.'

*'Yes, I usually am. Not tonight
though, I'm talking to you.'*

'Ok and how do you like it so far?'

*'I already feel you're a very special
person, Giuliana.'*

Smooth. She thought. She went along with it.

'Me too.'

*'So, what does your hubby say about
your chatting?'*

'Oh, he doesn't mind. He knows that

I don't go further than that.'

*'Oh, you've never met anyone you chat
with?'*

No. I only see them in their pictures.

That's it.'

> *'Oh, not even the webcam?'*

No.'

> *'Do they ask you out?'*

She already knew that he would do the same.

'Oh yes, many times.

They can get very insisting too,

but I tell them straight up

that I'm not interested.'

There, she thought, she told him too.

> *'Good for you. Do you have a picture,*
> *Giuliana?'*

'Sure, do you want to see it?'

> *'I'd like that…yes.'*

She was sure he would. She clicked on send file, attached the small photo she had scanned and sent it to him.

'Ok, it's coming.'

'Thanks. I'll send you mine as well.'

'Ok, thanks.'

After a few minutes, she got the message saying that her file had been sent. She also got a message that there was an incoming file for her. She opened it and saw two men with wine glasses in their hands. One was taller and darker than the other who was oriental.

'That's me on the left; the other man is the President of our company. We were at an award dinner.'

For a man his age, he wasn't so bad she thought.

'Did you get mine?'

'Yes, I did. It's pretty small but I can see those beautiful eyes. You certainly don't look 42. I wouldn't give you more than 35. I like the pose you're in too. Very sexy.'

Boy, he was smooth, but she really liked his reaction. Like every woman, she loved being told that she looked younger than her age.

'I love your compliments.

Thank you.

You don't look so bad yourself,

for a grandfather.'

She had to tell him something nice in return.

> *'Very kind of you, Giuliana. Your
> hubby is a very lucky man. He has
> you to hold every night!'*

'You may think that,

but unfortunately,

he takes me for granted.'

> *'He does? That's not good. Why is
> that?'*

'Well, you know how it is.

After so many years of marriage,

romance gets lost along the way.

What can you do, that's life!'

> *'No more romance? What a pity. He
> doesn't know what he's missing.'*

'I know. I tell him all the time that

sooner or later something will

happen so he shouldn't be too

surprised when it does. I told

I that I want to have more fun;

I want to go out more because

life is short. Right?'

> *'I agree with you, Giuliana. You*
> *sound like you crave romance, do you?*

'Oh yes, I do. Very much so.

Let me tell you, if the right

person came along, I would

consider a little romance on the side.

Are you romantic, Aaron?'

> *'Romantic: It was the most romantic*
> *place where two people can meet, as I*
> *watched her enter the dimly lit room.*
> *Her flimsy black dress swaying to the*
> *style of her sensual walk, her eyes*
> *gleaming and her skin a golden sheen*
> *which looked so precious. Our eyes met*

38

*as she passed me and the romance
within me exploded like a volcano, the
lava that spilled through it being the
heartfelt pleasures of romance. We
danced as I looked into her bright eyes,
not saying so much in words but looks
said it all. Then I woke
up............ahhhh.'*

Giuliana was shocked. Never had any of her buddies
written something like that for her. She was beginning to like
this man. A lot.

'Wow that was amazing.

You're very talented and romantic.'

'You really liked it?'

'Yes. You have talent.'

*'Ok. Then give me another word,
Giuliana.'*

'Ok. Let me think...touch.'

*'Touch: The human touch, tracing
your skin with the fingertips, erupting
feelings that we so locked up deep
within you. This is the true vibrating*

39

effect of Touch! A touch that makes you feel that you are alive, when your feelings move your world, take you into the thoughts of fantasy. A carnival of events turning around with bells and whistling chiming in the distance. A sensual touch can bring these virtues of life so much alive. So, let's touch .... how's that?'

'Amazing! You're really good.

Are you a writer?'

'No, I just express myself like this when I have the chance. Another word, Giuliana.'

'Oh, Ok. How about...kiss.'

'Kiss: As our lips brushed each other's the chemistry compelled our lips to meet, searching so breathlessly. Our bodies pressed on the dance floor and our minds wandered into a world where we wanted to be just alone. The first kiss seemed like an eternal flame. The warmth, the wetness, the

entangling of tongues - all reached a
dimension that two people in love can
only dream of. This we experienced as
we faded into an endless time, a world
where we longed to be, in a cloud that
wandered through life with no return.
mmmm what a kiss.........'

Giuliana was mesmerized by these pieces of poetry. She felt a tingling all over. She had never experienced anything like this on chat. She decided to copy his words onto a word document so she could print it out and keep it in a private place.

'Oh my. You're so good.

I'm copying your paragraphs into

a word document so I can read

them in private, later on.

Do you mind?'

'Of course not. That's very flattering.
Give me another word, baby.'

'All right. Let's try...embrace.'

'As I held her close in a warm

embrace I felt her heartbeat on mine. It was our first time, but we felt no shame, we felt a closeness that we longed for so much deep within us. Our embrace grew into one that we both thought would never go loose. It was something so special, so real, and so vibrating. We held each other closer with our embrace multiplying its strength, both wanting each other so much, feeling the beat of one another's heart which chimed within us. In this deep embrace we moved into the world of ecstasy, both wanting it in the most romantic, sensual manner that took us to heights we never thought existed. I watched her fall asleep in this same embrace... ahhhh'

'My goodness, you're so talented.

Are you sure you don't write

novels on the side?'

'Yes, baby. I'm really on a roll, tonight. Another word, please.'

'Ok, try love.'

'The love that emitted from her sensual words, her chemistry through this cyber medium reached a place in my heart that I never knew existed. A place barricaded for so long. For this I feel the love, the feelings of sensuality. To hold her close, to feel her heartbeat on mine, whisper sweet nothings that all blended into a Love that will surround two people that met so mysteriously. I know this can be illusion, but if two human beings want something like love to erupt... nothing seems impossible. I shall dwell in this thought tonight. How's that baby?'

Aaron was getting very interested to Giuliana now. Dangerously interesting.

'That was great! You are so good!'

'So are you. Thanks. You know, Giuliana, I'm feeling that something has begun between us. Do you feel the same? You're a very interesting woman and I would love to meet you in person,

43

would you like that too?'

There it was! The famous question. This time, though, was different. She did feel the same for him and she did want to meet him in person too. What was she thinking! This went against all her morals and all that she sustained to her other buddies.

'Yes, I do.'

There, it was done. She was curious now to see what came next.

> *'Really? Oh, you've made me very happy, tonight! This is my email, Giuliana. Let's not loose contact, ok? Aarong@aandf.com. Can I have yours too, please?'*

'I'm glad I did.

So have you. Here's mine,

Giulianam@hotmail.com'

> *'Great. I'll send you an email so we can organize an encounter, ok? I'll be away for a few days on a business trip, but I'll organize something when I get back. Do you have a different picture*

44

of yourself, Giuliana?'

'Yes, would you like me to send it?'

She had totally forgotten about exchanging pictures.

'Of course I do, please.'

'Okay. Wait a few minutes.'

'I'm not going anywhere.'

Giuliana sent him a different picture this time. After a few minutes the file was 100% sent.

'Got it, Giuliana, thanks. I'm going to send you another picture too.'

She received his file and opened it. This time it was only him on a golf course. He had his hands raised in the air like a celebration.

'You know, Giuliana, you're really appealing, and I like that pose. Did you receive my picture?'

'Yes, I did thanks. You like golf?'

'Yes. I had a great game that day and one of my business colleagues shot it.'

She knew it and she was satisfied with her guess. He

looked very happy in that picture.

Well, I'd better be heading

for bed now.

We'll chat soon, ok, Aaron.'

> *'Yes, you're right. It's getting very late now. So, would you consider meeting when I get back from my trip?'*

At this point, she would have wanted to see him now.

'Sure, why not. Just send me

an email when you get back. Ok.'

> *'That's great. Ok, well, sweet dreams and don't forget me, Giuliana.'*

He was so happy that she didn't refuse his offer.

'No, I won't forget you, Aaron.'

No, she wouldn't have, that was for sure.

CHAPTER FIVE

A few days passed and Giuliana decided it was time to follow up with Aaron. Was he back? Did he really mean what he said that night? Did he still remember her? She sent him an email during her lunch hour.

<u>May 30</u>

Hello Aaron,

How are you? Do you remember me? Are you OK? I haven't heard from you in a while. When you read this email, could you please resend me your picture at this address so I could save it? Sorry, I lost the one you sent me on chat.

Ciao

Giuliana

~~~~~~

Hello Giuliana,

I'm fine. Busy, as usual. Of course, I remember you. How could I forget? Yes, I will send you my picture again, as soon as I have the chance.

Take care,

Aaron

So, he didn't forget her after all. Giuliana was very pleased.

June 4

Hi Giuliana,

Sorry I could not reply earlier. I have been travelling and just came back from the U.S. Was a quick trip to sort out a problem with a big customer?

Anyway, hope you are keeping well, and everything is going well.

Take care Giuliana.

Regards

Aaron

~~~~~~

Hi Aaron,

Everything is great. My new job is going well. I can't complain.

Ciao

Giuliana

~~~~~~

Giuliana,

Did you get my picture? I sent it to you to this address as you asked me to.

Take care,

Aaron

~~~~~~

Hi,

Yes, I did. Thanks. Very handsome indeed! So, how's your day going so far?

Ciao

Giuliana

~~~~~~

Great! Since you sent me your email. Tell me, Giuliana, would you have time to meet with me. I would love to meet you in person. Just for a coffee or a drink. What about you?

Aaron

He didn't forget about her, and he remembered that he wanted to meet her, but she was on the fence about meeting him.

Hi,

Boy, I've never met anyone I chat with…but you sound so trustworthy…ok…why not.

Giuliana

Trustworthy. Now that was a careful woman.

Wow, thanks. Let's meet at Maple Leaf Shopping Mall in Brampton. There's a Tim Horton's for sure near there or maybe we could have a bite to eat. Whatever you want, Sweetie.

Aaron

Giuliana's hands were shaking when she typed up the next words.

Hi,

Ok, what time?

Giuliana

~~~~~~

Wonderful!

How about seven. In front of The Bay. I'll be in a silver Lexus.

Aaron

~~~~~~

Hi,

Seven is fine. I'll be wearing black. See you there.

Giuliana

~~~~~~~

My dear,

I can't wait.

Aaron

It was true. He really couldn't wait to meet this woman. He was already attracted to her, perilously attracted to her. He was going to meet her in a few hours and there was no turning back.

It was raining again. Giuliana decided to wear her black suit, the one she always wore to interviews. She thought that this was sort of an interview as well. Underneath she wore a very transparent, cream color, blouse so her new, French lace, bra which was visible to the eye. Hopefully, his eye. If she was hot, then she would take it off. The suit was getting pretty big on her now, but it still looked elegant for an evening encounter. She slowly and meticulously put on her make-up; a couple of drops of perfume and off she went.

She told Rocco that she was going to a going away party at work. He didn't mind, it wasn't the first time she went out with the girls, but it was the first time she lied about it.

On her way to the mall, she kept checking herself in the rear-view mirror. She wanted to look perfect for him. She was very anxious to meet this man and she was also wondering if he was just as anxious as she was. After what seemed an endless amount of time, she arrived in the mall parking lot and headed towards The Bay. There she parked her car, locked it, and started heading towards the mall doors. While she was walking, she was also scanning the parking lot in search of a silver Lexus.

Aaron was driving slowly in the parking lot. He was tightly holding on to the searing wheel and his knuckles were turning white. He was very anxious and was wondering what this woman was like in person. Sure, on the net they were all okay but in person the story changes.

When he made a left turn into the next lane, he saw her. She was walking towards him and when she recognized the car she smiled. Wow! He thought. She was really something. She was walking with her head up high, and she didn't seem nervous to him at all or she was hiding it very well. He liked what he saw so far.

There was the Lexus! It was him! She recognized him from the picture. She smiled when she realized that he had recognized her too. He opened the door for her.

"Hi. Aaron?"

"Yes, Giuliana. Come in, please." Her eyes were as dark as the night, her lips were a luscious cherry red, and her smile lit up her face. What a beautiful woman, he thought. She was full and round, and he would have loved to hug her right now. "Nice to finally meet you. Boy, you look great!" He said, as she made herself comfortable in the passenger seat, he took her hand and kissed it. He couldn't take his eyes off her, so he tried to keep his eyes on the road.

A kiss on the hand! Giuliana never experienced anything like that. He certainly was much better in person than the photo he sent her through email. He had a light East Indian accent and a deep voice. She found it very sexy. A pleasant surprise. "Thanks, you're not so bad yourself." She noticed that he was scanning her from head to toe. She blushed and chuckled to herself.

"So, where to you want to go, Sweetie?" He was trying very hard to keep his eyes on the road.

"Oh, it doesn't matter to me. You pick." Her heart was pounding so fast that she felt it was going to blow up. What was happening to her?

"I'm not too familiar with this area so I'll let you decide."

"Well, I know this area pretty well. I came to many interviews here. Do you just want to have coffee, or did you want to have a bite to eat?" She needed food. She always gets hungry when she gets excited.

"Sure, let go to dinner. Are there any good restaurants around here?" He also enjoyed listening to her voice, it was very sensual.

"Well, there was a really good Italian buffet, but they closed it down. I guess they were losing business. Let me think…just keep on this road and when we hit Steeles Avenue, you'll make a right.

As he continued driving, he was talking about himself. He was telling her how busy he was with work. He told her about an upcoming trip to Vienna and his business meetings in Cambridge and London. He felt he could loosen up with her. She was making him do that. She made him feel at ease and aroused at the same time.

Giuliana just sat there, looking at him and paying close attention to him. He was a very fascinating man. She noticed that he stuttered a bit, which reminded her of her son, Gabriele. It was probably the same kind of stuttering. When Gabriele got nervous, he stuttered. She chuckled. She also began to feel relaxed as she was pointing the way to the restaurant.

When they arrived, it was starting to rain again. Aaron flew out and hurried around to open the door for her. Magically, he had an open umbrella ready for her.

"A gentleman! Well, there aren't too many of those around anymore. Thank you, sir." She was stunned.

"You're welcome, Sweetie. I've always treated my women right."

"I like it when you call me Sweetie." She said it very softly so he could barely hear it. "Women?" She turned and looked at him raising her eyebrow.

He smiled and said:

"I mean with the lovely ladies."

She thought that he probably did have many women, gallant and suave as he was.

She was walking in front of him. She turned and gave

him the sexiest look. Aaron was watching her from behind. She had a very important walk, and he couldn't stop looking at her behind swaying back and forth. He was captivated.

As they had dinner, Giuliana began talking about herself now and Aaron was paying close attention. She talked about her children, her husband and her parents. She told him that she had just moved into a new home, and she described it to him. She pulled out her photos from her wallet and showed them to him. She had pictures of her husband, her kids at different ages, her sister, her niece, her nephew and a picture of herself when she was in high school.

"You know, Giuliana, you haven't changed much since high school. I find you look much better, though."

"Thank you." She was blushing. He could see that even under her make-up. "What do you mean by better?"

"Well, I mean, more mature, more woman, more sexier, more…"

"Ok, I get it. I get it. You're over flattering me, you know." She was blushing again as she looked down, trying to hide it.

Aaron also took out a picture. He showed her his son Terry, who was in pose with his wife, Megan and his daughter Virginia. She noticed that Megan was white as snow with long blonde hair and what seemed like blue eyes. Virginia was a lovely mixture of both of them. Aaron looked at the picture one more time, smiled and put it back in his wallet. He didn't pull out any more pictures. He probably didn't want Giuliana to see anyone else he was close to, like his wife.

Giuliana got the message, loud and clear. She didn't want to see his wife, anyway. She was sure that she would be comparing herself to his wife and she didn't want that right now. She wanted to enjoy the moment.

"Boy, it's hot in here." She wasn't really feeling warm, but she took her jacket off anyway and laid it over the back of the chair.

Aaron watched closely as Giuliana took her jacket off. He could see her bra under her transparent blouse. It was white lace and he also enjoyed seeing what full breasts it contained.

He couldn't take his eyes off them, and Giuliana noticed it.

"Oh, that's better." She said as she sat back down. She was really enjoying flirting with him.

"Oh yes, much better indeed." Aaron was aroused now. He hadn't felt this way about a woman in a long time. He would have certainly wanted to take her in his arms, right now. Control. He had to control himself, so he excused himself and went to the men's room.

Giuliana knew perfectly well what the effect of what she just did would have had on Aaron. She knew that certain actions made by a woman had certain effects on a man. Why was he so different? As Aaron excused himself for the men's room, she said:

"Sure, I'll wait right here." And chuckled as he went past her.

As Aaron entered the men's room he had to stop and catch his breath. What was happening to him? As he reached the sink, he said to himself.

"You fool!" He threw some water on his face, dried and

recomposed himself again. He went back to their table.

They finished dinner and Aaron asked for the bill. When the waitress returned with his receipt, he asked Giuliana if she wanted to leave.

"Okay, let's go." She said as she got up. Aaron quickly got up and picked up her jacket and opened it for her so she could wear it. She smiled at him, as he got a little closer to her so he could smell her perfume, which was spell bounding, yet very feminine. Giuliana felt his breath on her neck. Her panties suddenly became damp as a shiver ran down her spine.

"So, tell me, Giuliana. I hope you know your way back; you'll have to guide me." He noticed that it was starting to rain again.

"Oh, yes. Don't worry, Aaron, I know my way around. Ah, I can't believe this weather! Is summer ever going to come this year?" She said as she opened her compact umbrella.

"Have a little bit of faith, Giuliana, it will." As he opened his car door for her, he noticed that she lifted her skirt a bit as she lowered herself into the car seat. He felt it again! How could it be that this woman had this effect on him?

"I hope you're right." She said as he closed the door for her and made his way to the driver's seat. She pulled her skirt down and made herself comfortable for the trip back to the mall parking lot. She felt much better now than when she first got into his car.

As they made their way back to the mall, they talked about many things, including music, who they chat with online, Aaron's work, Giuliana's new job and her children. He gave Giuliana his business card and she gave him hers.

They arrived in the mall parking lot and Aaron asked where her car was parked. She showed him a red minivan and he parked right next to it. He turned off the motor and moved himself sideways so he could get a good look at her. She had become suddenly very quiet and was looking straight ahead. Aaron noticed that she was blushing. He enjoyed that very much because it made him feel young. Very young.

Giuliana noticed that Aaron had turned himself towards her and she knew why. Would he have the guts to kiss her on a first date? She would soon find out. Aaron didn't move but he placed his hand on her shoulder, very lightly. She could barely feel it, but she did feel it. They talked a little while longer and Giuliana looked at her watch.

"Wow did time fly! I'd better be heading off." She didn't want to go.

"Okay, then. I had a great time. Did you?" He wanted so much to kiss her but instead he took her hand, and he kissed it.

"Yes, I did. Thanks Aaron." He kissed her hand, again! This was probably the kiss she was getting for tonight. He was so noble and so adorable. She was really beginning to like this man. A lot.

She touched his arm and squeezed it, in a gesture of *Good Bye*, opened the door and headed towards her car.

"So did I. Goodbye…Giuliana…" He managed to say that as Giuliana let herself out. "Sweetie…" She didn't hear that.

As Giuliana was driving home her mind was going just

as fast as she was. "Stop it, Giuliana!" She said to herself out loud. "He's only a man, for God's sake! You met him online. It'll never work out!" Thank God, nobody could hear her. They would think she's gone mad. She was sure that she was.

Aaron was listening to the music full blast as he headed home. Wow. This woman already had such an effect on him. He hadn't felt this way for such a long time. Actually, he couldn't even remember when he felt this way for a woman, not even when he was dating his wife. All he was able to do with Vivian was get her pregnant. That was the biggest mistake of his life and he's still paying for it. Then there was Gilda. He remembered her at that moment. She was really insatiable and passionate. Lately, though, he was ready to leave Vivian. Maybe he was going through the mid-life crisis that most men go through when they reach the fifty-year mark or maybe this spark from this Italian woman lit up his virility again. He didn't know exactly but he sure felt different after he met Giuliana. That he did know.

Later that night

Dear Giuliana,

It was indeed a pleasure spending time with you today. I liked everything about you, and I was glad we enjoyed each other's company.

I hope you felt the same.

Look forward to seeing you again soon, if you would like that.

Take care and you looked great.

Regards

Aaron

CHAPTER SIX

Good Morning!

I agree with you about yesterday and yes, I would like to meet again. So, go on your trip and we'll talk later.

So, tell me, what did you like about me in particular?

Thanks for your compliments; they always make me feel good.

Ciao

Giuliana

~~~~~~

Morning Giuliana,

I am glad you felt the same.

What I liked particularly about you was your open nature, your smile, to say the least the 'whole package'. I can see you smiling? Am I right?

The whole package! Oh, she liked that. She sure was smiling all right and blushing too. His email continued:

If we walk through life with an open mind, everything you see, everything you touch or feel seems like a gift from God.

Virtues that have been bestowed on us all to enjoy the thrills and spills of whatever may come your way. It is up to us individuals to see through the beauty on this earth. Each person is so different, but yet made in each one's likeness.

To share thoughts and feelings, to share life's adventures and to get a mirror image and see that at the end of the day all of us are just the same in every perceivable sense. No cast, no creed, no color, no language can ever be regarded as a boundary to the human link. These are just man made.

So, walking through life with an open mind, an open concept in your heart can only lead us to the pangs of reality that the heart makes us feel…this is the only true organ which can be used as a barometer to the term of life that each of us is entitled to.

In the light of the above, what other feelings can I as a human being feel towards another? Only love, sensuality and the exchange of human aura fulfilling our needs with the beat of every heartbeat … this is how I see life and others that come into my life.

Hope this makes sense Giuliana.

Aaron

~~~~~~

Hi,

Yes, it does. A lot. You are such a good writer, you know.

Giuliana

She loved his writing and couldn't get enough of it.

<u>June 6</u>

Good morning!

How's your morning going? I'm swamped but I'm not complaining, I love it!

I am sending you this email using my work address. Hope you don't mind. I can keep track of my emails better this way. If you have something private to say, just send it to my Hotmail.

Ciao

Giuliana

~~~~~~

Hi Giuliana,

Thanks for thinking of me. I was thinking of you just a while ago.

I am having a busy morning too but taking it by stride.

I hope we can meet again before I leave on the 12th of June.

Would you like that?

Take care.

Aaron

Yes, she would! More than he would ever know.

Hi Aaron,

Quick reply. I'm in between tasks, being a multi-tasker!

Sure, we could meet. I'm not available on Monday or Tuesday.

We could try that movie on Sunday or tomorrow night. Your choice.

Ciao

Giuliana

~~~~~~

Hi Multi-tasker!

Thanks for your 'quickie'…

Maybe tomorrow evening might work.....so let me keep in touch and make out a plan to sneak out!!!! :)

Take care.

Aaron

Quickie! She didn't mean that, but she knew what Aaron meant.

You BAD boy!

If you can't let me know by the end of today, just leave me a message on my cell. [416-787-9966]

Ciao

Giuliana

~~~~~~

Sweetie

How about if I let you know by email tomorrow? Is that okay. By this evening, I would not know.

Thanks

Aaron

She couldn't get enough of being called 'Sweetie'.

Hi,

Ok, sure. I'll check my Hotmail tomorrow.

Ciao

Giuliana

Giuliana checked her Hotmail later that evening.

G:

If I can work it out how much time do you have? This is because I will make an excuse that I am going to the Racetrack which should bring me back home after 12 pm. So let me know, please.

Thanks Sweetie.

Aaron

Giuliana chuckled to herself. He sounded like a modern day, male Cinderella.

Hi,

Ah, just like Cinderella! That's so sweet.

I think we can catch a movie and be home before midnight…what do you think Prince Charming?

Giuliana

Aaron's laugh sounded very loud in his office. She's beautiful and funny. What more could he want?

No Sweetie, you misunderstood. I have to kill time after midnight because she knows when I do go to the racetrack, I return round about 1 or 1.30 a.m. That's what I meant.

I have to make it look real, and I cannot hang around until so

70

late doing nothing.

Aaron

~~~~~~

Oh, OK, sorry.

I don't have any problems with time…so make whatever you want of tomorrow night. Just tell me where and when.

Ciao

Giuliana

How about here and now.

Wow… sounds exciting.

Aaron

She could feel the excitement in his voice.

Now, now…don't get too excited!

Ciao

Giuliana

~~~~~~~

I did not sweetie…just said it 'sounds' exciting, that's all.

Nothing can be exciting unless it's a two way street! :-)

Aaron

~~~~~~

I agree!

Ciao G.

~~~~~~

'Great minds think alike.'

Till tomorrow night, we'll meet where we met last time, ok.

Aaron

~~~~~~

Hi,

Sure, sounds okay. Same time?

Giuliana

~~~~~~

Yes, I can't wait. I'll leave you a message on your cell if I can't make it for whatever reason. Okay?

Aaron

Friday was such a long day. Aaron was in meetings the whole day. He tried very hard to keep his mind on his work but there were certain moments that his thoughts were for his 'Sweetie'. He was daydreaming of their next date. Would she want to kiss him this time or maybe something more? That was enough! He had to get back on track and listen to his representative's presentation.

Friday was long for Giuliana too. Her mind also drifted towards Aaron. Where was he going to take her? Were they going to dinner and then a movie? Would he want to take her to the theatre? What was she going to wear? She decided to stop at the mall on her way home.

She saw this dress at The Bay. It was black, knee length, very deep neckline and it was her size. Her new size. She wasn't a plus size anymore. She was starting to fit into regular sizes now. She decided to try it on. It was a perfect fit! It was revealing enough to show her figure but not too much. Sold!

Giuliana headed towards the lingerie department. She picked out a lace bra with matching underwear. She didn't try those on, if they didn't fit, she would return them another day.

As soon as she got home, she flew upstairs to her bedroom and into her bathroom. She locked the door and immediately tried on the new lingerie set. Again, it was perfect.

She took the black dress out of the bag and tried it on over the set. Wow, she looked great! She was so proud of herself for losing weight and she wasn't going to stop until she reached the desired weight. She took everything off and carefully placed the clothes back into the bag and hid the bag in the back of her closet. Rocco would never think of looking there. He never asked himself why his wife was spending a lot of money on herself lately. He is only noticing that his wife is losing weight and that she's starting to look the way she did when he met her. And that he liked.

When Aaron woke on Saturday morning, he was aroused. He knew very well what the cause of that was. He tried not to face his wife as he got up and headed for the bathroom. So, what was he supposed to do now? Masturbate? He hadn't done that in ages, and he wondered if he still remembered how.

When he was done, he went back to bed, and he noticed his wife. She was flush and grumpy. He leaned over and felt her forehead. Fever. She had a fever! Shit! There goes his date for tonight! Damn! What luck!

He got dressed, went down to the kitchen and poured her some orange juice. He went back upstairs and placed the glass on her night table. He was cursing to himself as he was searching for the thermometer.

It was fever, all right! Damn! Now, he had no choice but to cancel his date. He was hoping Giuliana wouldn't be too disappointed. He sure as hell was.

Giuliana was so excited that she tossed and turned the whole night. Rocco sexually satisfied her, but she was starting to find his lovemaking boring. She felt like a teenager on the day of her prom. She felt so good, so beautiful and so young.

Like every Saturday morning, she got up, took a shower, got dressed and came downstairs to breakfast with her kids. Rocco got up a little later to make espresso coffee for him and Giuliana. They have been sharing that special moment for a while now. She always loved his espresso, he put his heart into it. After breakfast and their usual Saturday morning chit chat, Giuliana told Rocco that she was supposed to go out with her friends from work that evening.

"Sure, go ahead. We'll just order Pizza as we usually do." He didn't think anything of it.

Giuliana went back upstairs to make her bed and she turned the computer on in the meantime. She clicked on her Hotmail and clicked her inbox. Naturally, Aaron's message was there, so she opened it.

Giuliana,

I can't make it tonight; my wife has the flu! Darn! I'm so disappointed because I really wanted to see you tonight! Darn! I'm so sorry, Sweetie.

We'll email on Monday. Try and have a good weekend.

Miss you,

Aaron

Darn wasn't the word that Giuliana used when she read the email. She was so disappointed that tears almost came to her eyes, but she swallowed them down, shut down the computer and tried to make the best of her weekend.

CHAPTER SEVEN

Good morning!

How's your wife?

Giuliana

Not that she cared much.

Hi Giuliana

Good morning. She got some antibiotics from our doctor. Turns out it was some kind of infection. Hope she is okay before I leave.

So, what's your plan for tomorrow?

I look forward to seeing you before I go. I wish you could have taken off early on Wednesday because I have a morning meeting and can get the afternoon off if I need to. How are you for it?

Take care.

Aaron

~~~~~~

Hi,

I'm glad to hear your wife is better.

I'm off work at 4:30. I can call home and say I'm working

overtime. I can't take any time off from work, you know, being new and all. This is all I can do.

Let me know.

Giuliana

She didn't give a damn about his wife, really, but she was glad to know that he wanted to see her before he left for Vienna.

Hi

That's on Tuesday or Wednesday Giuliana?

So, what did you do during the weekend? I was really glad to meet you and enjoyed the time we spent, though brief. I have to admit I almost kissed you! :-) I can see you smiling.

Aaron

He almost kissed her! She figured that out, but he was a real gentleman, so he wasn't. Giuliana was smiling and blushing.

Hi,

Wednesday is better. Tuesday is my Weight Watchers night. You can come pick me up here at work if you want.

Yes, I did smile.

Giuliana

He knew that she smiled because she knew he really wanted to kiss her that first night, but it just wasn't his style.

My Sweetie!

Sure, let's do that. Was the smile a positive one? :-)

Aaron

What a silly question. She had never heard of a negative smile.

Hi,

Isn't a smile usually positive?

Do you know how to get here?

Giuliana

~~~~~~

No, I don't Sweetie. So, you can email me the directions whenever you can. 4.30 should be fine to pick you up.

How much time do you have and what would you like to do sweetie?

Aaron

For him, she would make time. All the time he wanted,

but she decided not to tell him that.

Hi,

Well, you take the 401 west, exit at Hurontario Street, and turn left. When you reach Brittania Road [you'll see a Wendy's on the corner], make a right.

Second light, turn left. Look for a big white building with "Car Space" written on it. You can't miss it.

Again, if you have any problems, call me.

Ciao

Giuliana

~~~~~~

Thanks. Entered in my GPS.

What would you like to do and how much time do you have Giuliana?

Aaron

~~~~~~

Hi,

Surprise me!

Giuliana

There, answer that one.

Depends on what you want to be surprised with! :-):-)

Aaron

Naughty boy!

Hi,

Can you take me to Paris on your private jet? I would like that!

Giuliana

~~~~~~

Wow....would you settle to be in my arms instead...it's safer?

Aaron

Sure, she would. Definitely.

I'd prefer it safer but can I be safe in your arms while flying to Paris?

Giuliana

~~~~~~

How about we do both, baby? Would you be on that jet, fifteen thousand feet in the air, in my arms experiencing those sensual kisses we talked about?

:-)

Aaron

She looked around and was happy that nobody saw her turn red like a tomato.

Now you made me blush, just like a teenager!

Well, if I can't go to Paris, then you can organize the evening.

Giuliana

~~~~~~

:-):-) so seems to me you still prefer the 'jet' to being in my arms with those sensual kisses and....

:-) remember you told me we agreed on that and we both liked soooooooooo much... :-)

Over to you.... :-):-)

Aaron

It was very clear to Giuliana that he wanted more than just kissing.

I know, I know!

But being in Paris, this time of year...........romance,

shopping..............what more could a woman want!

Ciao

Giuliana

Well, she did have a right to dream, didn't she?

I know what you mean sweetie. I guess this is every woman's dream until they see the prices in Paris. It's mind boggling.

So, we can take ourselves to an imaginative height to Paris, if it's mutual!? :):) I can see you blushing sweetie.

Aaron

Did he have ESP or something like that! She was blushing, again!

You have good vision!

Giuliana

Certainly...my vision is fantabulous!!!! But I cannot read your mind...so you have to give me vision into your mind too. :):):) will you?

Aaron

~~~~~~

There's a lot of confusion in my mind right now, trust me, I can't even understand it. You'll have to give me more time for that. Okay?

Giuliana

That was true.

Sure, I do understand. No problem at all. I like mutual understanding as I told you so often.

Aaron

June 10

Good morning!

How's your day going?

Giuliana

~~~~~~

Hi

Good morning to you too. I am having a busy day, but somehow trying to get everything put in place before I leave on Thursday.

I hope I will succeed?

Aaron

~~~~~~

Oh, I'm sure you will. You're not the V.P. for nothing, right?

Giuliana

~~~~~~

Hi Giuliana,

You bet. Thanks for consoling me :):):)

Aaron

Aaron had two meetings to attend that day and couldn't email Giuliana back. He also had an important meeting the next day with an important client in Cambridge and therefore wouldn't have the time to meet Giuliana before he left. Once again, he was disappointed because he really wanted to make true what was said in those emails.

Being a very patient woman, Giuliana, emailed him the next day but there was no reply. She knew he had meetings to attend and lots of work to do before he left. She would try again tomorrow.

<u>June 12</u>

Today was the day that Aaron had to leave for Austria.

Good morning!

Are you there? What time do you leave?

Giuliana

~~~~~~

Hi Sweetie,

I have been in the office since 7.30 am again today. I will leave the office around noon. My flight is leaving late afternoon.

I am sure I should be able to get everything done before leaving.

Take care and talk to you soon.

Aaron

~~~~~~

Hi Aaron,

I'll bet you'll sleep all the way to Vienna, you must be very tired.

Anyway, you owe me a couple of missed dates, buddy! So, if you bring me a souvenir from Vienna, I'll forgive you. Okay?

Have a good trip and don't forget me.

Ciao

Giuliana

~~~~~~

Sweetie,

Yes, you're right! I owe you. I promise to make it up to you when I get back and I will buy you a little something so I can give it to you when we meet again.

Of course, I won't forget you, how can I?

Take care,

Aaron

Aaron had not been able to get her out of his mind since that late night they met online. He marveled at how she stole his heart immediately.

~~~~~~

Even though she couldn't get Aaron off her mind, the week passed as usual for Giuliana. Her kids were out of school now and they were beginning to enjoy their summer vacation. She was always a bit nervous when the kids were home by themselves in the summertime, but they were also getting older, and they could handle themselves perfectly. She stocked up the freezer with microwave dinners and plenty of drinks, so at least they wouldn't starve while she and Rocco were at work.

Across the pond, Aaron's trip was going very well. Vienna was such a beautiful city, so antique yet modern at the same time. It reminded him of when he was living in Holland. He would have loved to have Giuliana there; it would have been a very romantic week. He knew that she needed to be wined and dined but she was back in Canada, and he missed her terribly. He took the opportunity to do some sightseeing in the evening. He also bought some souvenirs for his wife and his granddaughter. He also found something special for Giuliana, but he would have to hide it very carefully because if Vivian found it, she would keep it for herself, and he couldn't explain that it wasn't meant for her.

CHAPTER EIGHT

<u>*June 25*</u>

Giuliana couldn't wait to hear back from Aaron so as soon as her email was turned on, she emailed Aaron.

Good morning, Aaron,

Welcome back! How was Vienna?

Giuliana

~~~~~~

Good morning my sweet Giuliana,

Thanks for your email sweetie. I returned Saturday evening. I went to a party three hours later and came back at three in the morning. On Sunday I went to Ajax for a family affair and then I spent some time with my lovely granddaughter, Virginia.

Vienna was so good. It's the most romantic city in the world, hands down. I always love it there...Paris takes a back seat when it comes to Vienna. It's so full of allure and history. I loved it. I golfed on the weekend of my arrival, but it was so hot, it was abnormal.

Hope you are enjoying this good weather...see you soon.

Aaron

What stamina he had. He certainly can pack his days with activities.

Hello again,

Boy, you've been busy! I guess it's normal for you. You must be tired though...with the jet lag and all.

Yes, you told me about your granddaughter, and you showed me a picture too...remember?

I sure would have loved to have been in Vienna with you...the romance cure could do me well.

Yes, I am enjoying the weather. I am going for walks every evening...usually alone. I went to the movies with the kids yesterday, saw The Hulk. What don't we do for our kids?

Ciao

Giuliana

~~~~~~

Hello again!

It's nice to be back, and it's nice to be exchanging emails with you of course.

I am glad you are doing what you enjoy Giuliana. As I told you when we met, I believe that everyone should follow their heart and not deprive it of anything at all. Life is too short for that. Every time I go out and come back, I believe in this concept more and more.

So how are you placed this week?

Let me know.

Aaron

~ ~ ~ ~ ~ ~

Hi,

Yes, I agree with you about following your heart and you're also so right about life being short. Therefore, I'm going to enjoy as much as I can of it.

Having said that...I can't make it today or tomorrow, but Wednesday, Thursday and Friday are ok.

Let me know.

Giuliana

~~~~~~

Hi,

Sounds good. Let me see what day would fit in best. Any

restrictions on time available and if so which day, Wednesday,

Thursday or Friday?

Take care,

Aaron

~~~~~~

Hi,

No problems with time.

Let me know.

Ciao

Giuliana

She would always find time for him. She was curious to know how he was physically; how were his kisses, his caresses. Patience.

Sure, I will Giuliana. I'm trying to work something out. I will try for Friday with no time restriction, but maybe we can also meet on Wednesday or Thursday for about 45 minutes or so if you would like that?

Take care,

Aaron

~~~~~~

Hi,

Yes, I would. Friday sounds good too.

Let me know.

Giuliana

~~~~~~

Sure, I will sweetie. Mind me calling you 'sweetie'? :)

If I can plan something for Friday, what would you like to do??

Aaron

Yes! Yes! Yes! And yes, of course he could call her sweetie.

Hi,

You've been calling me 'sweetie' many times now, have I ever objected?

I really don't know what I would like to do for Friday. Why don't you surprise me? You certainly know your nightlife better than me.

Ciao

Giuliana

~~~~~~

Hmmmm, yes, I have been calling you sweetie many times, and you know you are the only one I call 'sweetie'. So, I thought I would just re-assure myself this is okay with you!!!!!

For Friday let's see if my plan works and I will see what we can do.

Just for curiosity sake, what time would your hubby expect you back??

Well, anyway let's see what we can organize for Friday.

Aaron

~~~~~~

Hi,

I didn't know that you only called ME sweetie, I like that.

The only time he would get suspicious is if I don't return home at all...lol...but if we make the wee hours of the night, he wouldn't mind. I've advised him that I intend to have a social life, with or without him.

So, there you go.

Ciao

Giuliana

~~~~~~

Hi,

Okay that's fine with me. I will do everything possible and somehow make up a plan. Look forward to it for sure! Do you?

:)

Let's try and meet on Wednesday or Thursday for a chat/coffee!!!!

Take care, XXX

Aaron

Again, there were no more emails. He probably had another meeting. It was ok, there was tomorrow.

<u>*June 26*</u>

Good morning, Aaron,

How are things? I'm already having a busy morning but it's okay.

Ciao

Giuliana

~~~~~~

Good morning, Sweetie,

Nice to hear from you. Somehow you have become somewhat special, and I do look forward to your emails! I must also thank you so much for thinking of mA, because that's very important to me. You do have a way about you sweetie, and I love it...believe me.

I started the day with a problem. One of my shipments destined to the USA had been miss-labelled by the producer and it drove me up the wall early morning. Thanks to your email I was able to smile again!

Look forward to seeing you tomorrow. I wish you had the chance to take off around 2 pm or so, but I do understand your situation.

Hope you have a good day sweetie....

Here is a hug and a kiss for the day....

XXXXXOOOOO

Aaron

~~~~~~

Hi,

I'm glad that I have this effect on you, and I hope your problem is solved now.

So please remind mA, when are you coming tomorrow? Are you coming to pick me up from work?

Let me know.

Giuliana

~~~~~~

Sweetie,

Yes, I can do that. What time are you off Giuliana? And give me the directions again from the 401 or 407.

Aaron

~~~~~~

Hi,

I'm off at 4:30.

From the 401, exit on Hurontario, turn left, first light is Britannia Road, make a right, at the second light make a left. You'll see a big, white building with "Car Space" on it. You can't miss it.

Ciao

Giuliana

~~~~~~

Hi,

Thanks sweetie. Any chance of getting off at 4 pm? This will give us a bit more time together. If not that's ok.

Aaron

~~~~~~

Hi,

Time is not an issue.

Can we text from now on? It would be faster.

Giuliana

~~~~~~

Oh, darling, I'd love that, but my wife is very nosy, and she would find them right away. Would you mind emailing dear? It's safer.

~~~~~~

Oh, of course. I had no clue. I'm sorry.

Emailing it is. She certainly didn't want to get him into any trouble.

<u>June 27</u>

Good morning!

Boy what a busy morning! How's your day so far?

Ciao

98

Giuliana

~~~~~~

Good morning to you too!!!!!!

After a fifteen-minute meeting with my sales staff, it's been oddly quiet.

Giuliana, I will be able to leave the office today only around 4.30 pm. Which means I can meet you between 5.15 and 5.30 pm is that ok sweetie? I have an unexpected meeting at 3.30 pm in the office.

Where would you like to meet? Please let me know.

Take care.

Aaron

~~~~~~

Hi,

Busy, busy! That's OK. I'll do some shopping in the meantime. We can meet at Tim Horton's which is on the corner of Brittania Road and Hurontario. You'll see it when you get off the 401. I'll see you there.

Ciao

Giuliana

~~~~~~

There you go, Sweetie, now you have time to spend some money on yourself, Giuliana, with a shopping spree! :)

See you there. Give me your cell phone number again, please.

You have mine?

Aaron

~~~~~~

Hi,

I've been spending too much money lately. Nothing fits me anymore; everything is too big.

Anyway, its 416-787-9966. I have your cell number, it's on your business card. You gave it to me the first time we met. Remember?

Ciao

Giuliana

~~~~~~

Oh, how silly of me. Yes, I'll see you later.

Love,

Aaron

Giuliana couldn't wait for her workday to end. She had called home to tell her that she was going for a drink with some friends at work and she probably wouldn't be home for dinner.

Finally, it was 4:30. She shut down her computer, grabbed her purse and headed for the door. When she exited the building, Aaron's Lexus was outside parked in a free parking spot.

He didn't get out of the car to let Giuliana in because he didn't want anyone to see him. He was certain that every person coming out of that door would know that he wasn't Giuliana's husband and at that moment he was happy that his car had tinted windows. He saw her opening the door, a big smile lit up her face. She was wearing a flowered, knee Length skirt and pheasant type top with a very low neckline and high heeled sandals. Her hair was up, and she had little or no make-up on.

"Hello, Sweetie. You look fabulous! Boy, you're sexy! I'm sure that you must drive all those men you work with crazy!"

He said as he tried to kiss her, but she turned to give

him her cheek. He was aroused.

Did he just try to kiss her? Well, she didn't want anyone noticing while they were still at work.

"Oh, stop it! Is that all you have on your mind?" she said as she slapped him on the wrist. "The men I work with don't even give me half a look, trust me." She said as she turned to look at the door.

He started the car and made his way out of the parking lot.

"Take it from me, Sweetie, if you go to work like that every day, you're bound to get stared at. You probably don't notice it, that's all. Thank God, we don't work together, I wouldn't get any work done!"

That was the truth!

"True, neither would I." She changed the subject. "So, how are you, Aaron?" she said as she lightly stroked his arm. She could see that he felt it even through his jacket.

"I'm fine, now that I'm with you." He really meant that.

"Ah, you're so sweet, Aaron…I feel the same way too."

She also meant that too.

"So, where are we going, Sweetie?" he said as he was trying to pay attention to the road.

"Oh, just make a right at the light, see that little plaza over there…"

She was pointing to a little group of stores on the corner of the next intersection "there's a coffee shop there and they make a great espresso."

"Whatever you want, Sweetie. You're the boss!"

He said to her as he was following her instructions.

"Oh, I am, am I? Okay. Oooooh, I like being in control."

She gave him the sexiest look.

Aaron thought that she was already very much in control of him because she knew all the right buttons to push. She had a strange ability to calm his nerves while he became aroused. He's never felt like this with any woman. He parked the car, got out and went around to open the door for Giuliana. He gave her his hand and she held it as she got out, he squeezed it. What did that squeeze mean?

Giuliana was beginning to get used to his gentle ways. He rushed to open the shop door for her and as she walked in, he caressed her back in a way that she never experienced.

Aaron followed Giuliana into the coffee shop, keeping a slight distance so he could enjoy her swaying her hips back and forth. She mesmerized him. They made their way to the corner where there was a love seat. As they sat down, Aaron put his arm around Giuliana's shoulder, and she snuggled next to him.

"I really like this place and I love being here with you, Giuliana. You relax mA, you know?" He was rubbing her shoulder. "So, what would you like?" he asked as he let her go for the moment.

"A short, single espresso, thanks." she said as she crossed her legs and her arms across her belly.

"Anything you want, Sweetie." He said as touched her face with the back of his hand. "Gorgeous!" She had such soft skin. A few minutes later he was back with her coffee and an iced tea for himself. He set the drinks on the coffee table and sat himself next to her again and once again put his arm around her shoulder so she could once again snuggle next to him.

"There, aren't we cozy?"

"Yes, very." She sipped her coffee. "I always like the coffee here, they make it just the way I like it, short and strong."

Another couple of sips and her espresso was done, so she made herself comfortable again.

"So, tell me, Giuliana, what will you be doing for the long weekend?"

"Nothing much. I don't like going to the cottage and I have to work on Monday because I'm still so new that I can't afford to take a day off. I guess I'll just relax on Tuesday, that's all. The weather doesn't look promising anyway but at least the rest of the week will be short. What's going on with you?" She ran her finger up and down his arm which had a certain effect on him.

He stopped her and held her hand tightly. "Well, it's my granddaughter's birthday on Saturday, she's turning two. It's amazing, just the other day I was holding her in my arms and now she's already two." His eyes lit up when he spoke of his Virginia, he loved being her grandfather.

"Oh, yes. They grow so quickly! Just the other day it seemed they were just learning to walk and the day after tomorrow they'll be off to university. Time really flies. That's why I didn't have my children one after the other. They are four and five years apart so I could enjoy raising them."

"You can tell that you really love your children, your face lights up when you speak of them. That's another think I like about you, you're a very passionate woman. My wife is not like you at all, she's bland." Vivian could never arouse him with a touch like Giuliana was doing. He turned into an icicle when she touched him.

"Oh yes, I am very passionate, that's true. Wow, Aaron, you know me so well, that's amazing. I guess it comes from my Italian background." She was always told that she got her fired up personality from her father. A very passionate south Italian man.

Aaron moved closer to her so he could whisper in her

ear. "Are you passionate in bed as well?"

The hairs on Giuliana's neck became erect when he said that. She gave him a light elbow in his stomach. "Stop it! We're in public, they could hear us." But she gently moved his head so she could whisper in his ear this time. "You might find out soon enough."

God! He would have wanted to make love to her right there! He was so aroused that he thought he was going to come in his pants. He decided to change the subject.

"So, I think my son might want to celebrate Virginia's birthday tomorrow night because she was born in the evening, and he wants her to blow out the candles right at the hour of her birth."

"Oh, that's so sweet. I've never thought of that, it's a neat

idea."

She knew he was trying to change the subject, so she just played along.

"Yes, it is. It's becoming a tradition in our family."

Aaron had emptied his glass.

"Do you want something else, Sweetie?"

He asked her as he got up. She looked at her watch.

"Oh my, it's getting late. I can't believe how time flies!
Well, I guess it's because I'm having fun. No thanks, Aaron, I
think I'd best be going now."

She also got up.

"Ok, then, let's go…but before you go, come in my car
for a few minutes."

He couldn't let her go so quickly. He noticed that she
couldn't say no to him.

"Ok, but only for a few minutes."

As they left the coffee shop, Aaron opened the
passenger door for her. She settled herself in and he got in as
well. His car smelled of new and she loved that smell. She
passed her left hand on his leather seats and ended up on his
lap. He looked at her hand and looked at her face. She was
biting her lips. He couldn't resist her. He reached as far as he
could to place his lips on hers. She responded as he suspected

she would.

Aaron gently pushed her away and went into his jacket pocket to pull out a small gift. He handed it to her.

"Oh, what's this?" she asked.

"Just a little something from Vienna." He replied.

Giuliana quickly opened the box and inside she saw a silver chain with pendant that spelled "Vienna". Her eyes widened as she gently pulled out the necklace.

"Oh my God, Aaron, this is gorgeous!" She exclaimed.

She threw her arms around his neck and kissed him passionately. As he kept his lips glued to hers, he began to make his way to the top button of her silk blouse. He flipped the button out of the buttonhole.

"I thought I would bring a bit of Vienna to my Sweetie." He said while unbuttoning another two buttons.

She trembled at that gesture and felt her panties become wet. When he got to the fourth button, she couldn't continue. So, she stopped him from going any further.

"I'm sorry Aaron but I can't continue!"

He didn't want to stop. He was just getting started.

"But why my dear?" He asked.

She answered as she pushed back.

"Because this is neither the time nor the place. Please Aaron, perhaps we can meet again in a more private place?"

He understood. He didn't like it, but he understood. This woman was not a "make out in the back seat" kind of woman. Oh no. She wanted to do things right.

"Yes, of course we can." And gave her a big smile.

"Thank you! I'm so glad you understand!" She composed herself.

"I do but..." and he gently put two fingers under her chin and kissed lightly on her cherry red lips, "to be continued...yes?"

She gave him a very lewd smile.

"Yes of course." Then she patted his cheek in the most sensual way and got out of the car.

She then ran to her car and drove home as fast as she could without breaking the law.

CHAPTER NINE

Although it was Saturday morning, she fired up her computer and emailed Aaron in the hopes of a response.

Good morning, Aaron!

Another busy day, I assume.

So, what's it looking like for tonight? If you have your Granddaughter's Birthday tonight, it's okay. Family comes first.

We could try tomorrow, if you can get away.

Let me know?

Giuliana

~~~~~~

Good morning, Giuliana,

I am sorry I will be having a busy day. Most of the day, I'll be playing golf with my Account Managers and visiting customers.

Today looks bad indeed. The plan now is that my son wants us to come there tonight so they can celebrate her birthday just with the grandparents at the time she was born which is 9:45 pm Saturday. That's a tradition in the family and my son is starting it again. I like that.

Then Sunday will be a family celebration so it will be out for me. Someone else has made my plans this time! What can one do?

I am sorry Giuliana, but I will somehow plan something very soon and let you know. By the way I loved those kisses. I love sensual kissing, I told you. Made me want to go further but you stopped at the right time. Oh boy! Hmmmmmmmmm.....

Enjoy your weekend.

Aaron

~~~~~~

Giuliana was reassured that he still wanted her kisses because she also wanted his. And more.

Hi Aaron,

Okay, like I said in my previous emails, I'm getting used to this and I suppose we'll have to take whatever we can get. Let's try next weekend then.

About the other night, yes, I loved it too...maybe too much...I had to stop...something came over me...I don't know...I'm glad you're not angry because I left abruptly...I couldn't sleep last night as I kept feeling those kisses and those hands!

Ciao

Giuliana

As Aaron read her email, he thought back to that encounter. Boy, was she right about that moment. He would have certainly gone further if she hadn't stopped him.

Dearest Giuliana,

Thanks for your email. I'm really sorry that this weekend didn't work out...again...I guess this is what we have to expect based on the life we have chosen to lead. I enjoyed kissing you very much indeed and I loved the sensuality you showed. Our tongues collided. I was itching to go further, believe me.

The wandering of my hands was magnetic, and your touch was electrifying. Since you couldn't sleep, does that mean you wanted more?

At this point, I do want more, Sweetie, much more. There's no going back now.

I wasn't angry at you, not at all. You stopped me from carrying on in a public place and that would not have been ideal in that moment.

Love Aaron

~~~~~~

Giuliana's heart was pounding out of control as she thought back at their meeting. She wanted more, much more. She was ready for Aaron and all he had to offer.

Hi,

Yes, I would have wanted more. I want this. So, let's see where this takes us, okay? We can meet whenever you get a chance. I can make up an excuse at any time.

You're right, I was in the mood for more and that's why I left so suddenly. I couldn't go any further in the coffee shop. God...I was shaking all the way home!

Ciao, Giuliana

~~~~~~

Aaron was shaking all the way home too. So much so that he had a hard time concentrating on his driving.

Hi,

Sounds so positive and I love the feeling. Your last line brought a smile to my face. I'm glad I wasn't the one who said that "I was shaking all the way home." Ha Ha!

Take care, Aaron

~~~~~~

Giuliana didn't get what he meant.

Hi,

I'm a positive thinker and I'm glad you think that way. Why did you smile at my last line? So, sorry, I didn't get it.

XXX

Giuliana

Aaron was fascinated by her purity, he chuckled.

My darling,

Yes, I did but I could not have said 'I was shaking all the way home' you would have misunderstood...haha...

Your Aaron

Oh, now I get it! She laughed out loud. Shaking as in masturbating. She covered her mouth with her hand so nobody would notice her laughter.

Hi,

Now, I get it. I didn't realize you have a dirty mind...I was not thinking that at all! I want to than you though...for making me feel so young again...I feel like a teenager who has a new boyfriend. I haven't felt that in ages!

Thanks, Giuliana

Giuliana didn't know that Aaron felt the same way. He certainly didn't feel fifty-two when he was with her.

My darling Giuliana,

You are most welcome. It's good to feel that way and this absolutely rejuvenates you. I certainly look forward to seeing you soon, and this time I WILL kiss you more for sure. :) Would you like that?

If you do like it, maybe we can book a room one evening and spend some time together, with a bottle of wine. Where we don't have to look over our shoulders. Would you like that? If you do, please let me know. If you do not, I will understand. I should be able to make excuses from about five to nine or so on a working day. Let me know please? Hoping you'll say yes.

Aaron

Book a room! Boy, he was moving quickly. She had to admit, she already wanted it too.

Aaron,

As I said before, yes, I would love to spend time with you but getting a room? Isn't that a bit too soon? We've only met twice.

Oh, what the heck! She thought.

Oh heck, I want that too. Could you organize a business weekend? Is that doable?

Giuliana

She was confident that he would go for a business weekend. Now, that sounded like a good idea to her.

Sweetie,

Well, let's see. Even if nothing happens, it will be relaxing to do this few hours get-together. I think, because we don't have to look over our shoulders at any time, let's spend a few relaxing hours for now. I would like that very much. What do you say?

Aaron

He certainly was very insistent when he wanted something, but Giuliana felt she needed to slow him down a little.

Aaron,

As a woman, I have to play a little hard to get so I'll think about it…how's that sound?

Ciao Giuliana

Aaron wasn't giving up so easily.

Giuliana,

Fair enough, sweetie. No problem. I told you, I'm straight forward and no pressure. I only believe in a two-way street.

But just to entice you: imagine the kissing, cuddling, sensual touching, and if we like it from that point onwards, just imagine the rest…haha.

Your Aaron.

Neither was Giuliana.

Hi,

See, that's why we should wait.......all the better........don't you think?

Ciao

Giuliana

Touchè!

Giuliana,

OKAY gotcha! I think if two people want something it should be mutual...so sure let me know when you are ready. I respect that.

Should you change your mind also let me know.

Tell me Giuliana, what did you like most about our kissing and touching?

Aaron

Everything!

Aaron,

Oh, it was great...really...I felt desired.... wanted...guilty...passion...so many feelings!

118

Your turn...Ciao

Giuliana

~~~~~~

G,

Well... I felt the same.

The feel of your lips, your tongue brought forth sensations that took me into a cloud of need, ecstasy and want. There I dwelt for as long as it lasted. If I had closed my eyes, I would not have known that tomorrow dawns.

My hands did feel the sensitivity of your skin, the vibrant passion that erupted.

Well, wish it lasted a bit longer, but then again it was better the way the screen closed...

Take care,

Aaron

Giuliana closed her eyes for a moment so she could turn Aaron's words into a movie scene where she was the main protagonist.

<u>July 4</u>

Good morning, Aaron,

119

How's your day looking today? Hope you're not too busy.

Ciao

Giuliana

~~~~~~

Morning Sweetie,

So far so good. I am having more of a busy time at home since my wife's family is here from Germany and the U.S. People and kids all over the darn place! Driving me bonkers!

Anyway, I have to go through this till July 18th. I leave for Chicago on 12th of July....which is a relief.

Talk to you soon!

Aaron

~~~~~~

Hi,

So, what I'm reading through the lines is that we cannot meet until they're all gone?

Ciao

Giuliana

~~~~~~

She didn't receive a response until just before five.

Sweetie,

Please bear with me Giuliana, because yesterday was just another hectic day with staff meetings all afternoon. I had to sort out some problems with the staff and it really took all my time.

Then last evening as I went home my wife and her family wanted to go to 'Young Thai', downtown, and then we went for a walk on Yonge Street.

I was beat...but tagged along. We came back at 12.30 last night and then had to write a short proposal to a company in London who had a board meeting this morning. Finally, slept at 2 am. Then up at 6 am and in the office at 7.30 a.m. So, there you go!

Giuliana, please do not think that I do not have time, but these days have been so hectic, I did not even find time to have a bite until 3:30 pm.!

Hopefully next week will be better.

Take care,

Aaron

~~~~~~

Dear Aaron,

I really feel for you! I really don't know how you do it! You know by now that I'm patient, very patient. I'm happy that you have some time to answer my emails [at least].

Just don't overdo it, please. I just found you and I don't want to lose you so soon…okay?

Don't worry, next week is fine…just let me know.

If you get stressed at any moment and you want to hear my voice…just call me on my cell. I'll always be there for you.

Ciao

Giuliana

~~~~~~

Giuliana,

Thanks so much Giuliana. I knew you would understand and that's why I elaborated on things I generally do not discuss with anyone else.

Hmmmmm so you say you are impatient eh! Give me a hint on your impatience! :)

I enjoyed our brief meetings Giuliana, and for sure I recall the last meeting so well!

Take care,

Aaron

~~~~~~

Oh Aaron,

Read that email again, dear, I said I'm patient, but deep down, I can't wait to be in your arms...and you?

XXXXX

Giuliana

~~~~~~

G,

Thanks for your email. When you say that I remember our last meeting. So, this is good. Yes, I want that too. Come on, excite me more, ha ha!

Aaron

~~~~~~

Aaron,

If I get you too excited, then you'll have no choice but to come out and see me. Now, what do you want me to do?

XXXXX

Giuliana

~~~~~~

G,

Excite me..... :)!

A

~~~~~~

A,

Ok, but I'm not good with words like you........well if you can.....imagine that I'm walking in your office...right now....I'm closing the door....and I'm getting closer....

G

~~~~~~

G,

MMMM loving it... go on…

A

~~~~~~

A,

Okay, so, a big hello kiss, in the meantime your jacket is coming off...still kissing...but now you're touching me...ohhhhhh…right there!

G

~~~~~~

G,

WOW... you are exciting me. Go on!

A

~~~~~~

A,

Now, I'm undoing your tie...starting to unbutton your shirt...meanwhile...your hands are under my top...and all over me...your tie is on the floor along with your shirt...

G

~~~~~~

G,

Man, you are driving me nuts in here! So, what am I touching sweetie? Give me more details... I like that... :)

A

~~~~~~

A,

You're touching me all over...just imagine...oh I know you like it.

Clothes are piling on the floor…

G

~~~~~~

G,

Damn woman! Mmmm... getting better. Give me more...

A

~~~~~~

A,

Well....my dear...I have to leave it to your imagination because I really can't go on any further...you can only say so much on an email...right?

So, you really can't run down here to meet for an hour or so?

G

~~~~~~

G,

Damn! But I understand Giuliana... but it was nice, very nice!

Next week I will somehow find the time in the evening to spend some time together, okay.

A

~~~~~~

A,

Okay, but remember you promised.

Ciao

G

~~~~~~

G,

Yes, I did and yes, I will. It can be the 8th or 9th evening. Not sure yet but one of these days is sure. I might be able to get some hours after say 7 pm. Would it be okay for you?

This time we can kiss more and mmmmm, I loved that tongue sucking. Would you like more than that when we meet?? You have to tell me....

A

~ ~ ~ ~ ~ ~

A,

When we meet, you'll find out!

127

Ciao

G

She hoped that she was able to relieve some of his stress.

CHAPTER TEN

<u>*July 8*</u>

Good morning, Aaron,

Are you there today! I missed you yesterday!

Ciao

Giuliana

~~~~~~

Good morning to you, Sweetie,

Sorry, I had no access to email yesterday. I picked up a customer from the Airport and spent all day with him...got back home around 8.30 pm.

Today, I will have more time to reply to your emails.

Take care,

Aaron

~~~~~~

Hi,

I figured that out. Very important customer? And your relatives? Still driving you nuts?

Ciao

Giuliana

~~~~~~

Giuliana,

Yes, the customer I went out with was important for the future...and I always like to be hospitable, because it pays in the long run.

Relatives: yes, they are still here Giuliana. I think most of them will be gone by the 18th of July. Right now, it's late night and lots of chatting as usual.

I leave for Chicago on the 12th of July and back on the 16th. So it will be a peaceful time then...

Aaron

~~~~~~

Hi,

So, do you think it would be possible to meet this week? Remember you promised last Friday..........do you remember last Friday?

Ciao

Giuliana

~~~~~~

Giuliana,

I will do my best and that's for sure. I would certainly love to see you again after all the stress I am coping up with right now...... :)

Aaron

~~~~~~

Aaron,

God knows you deserve it! I wish we were closer so I could relieve your stress whenever you need it.

Too bad!

Ciao

Giuliana

~~~~~~

Thanks Giuliana,

I would love that.

Aaron

~~~~~~

A,

I know you would! So, would I.

XXX

Giuliana

~~~~~~

G,

So, we both do… :)

Aaron

~~~~~~

A,

There you go...all the more reason to free yourself for me.

Ciao

Giuliana

~~~~~~

Giuliana,

I will find time for sure. Once the rush is over during the daytime on Saturday is also another option...if you can make it of course.

Aaron

~~~~~~

Aaron,

Boy Saturday is so far away...but if there's no other choice.......okay.

Let me know.

Giuliana

~~~~~~

Giuliana,

What I mean is Saturdays in general...but in case I can get away on a normal day would short notice be okay? And can I contact you on your cell then? I'm just trying to get some ideas in place.

Aaron

~~~~~~

Aaron,

Okay, I understand...short notice is okay too...just let me know...through emails or cell, it's usually off but leave me a message, I always check my messages.

What ideas do you have in mind?

Ciao

Giuliana

~~~~~~

G,

What I mean is, whenever I get the chance to scoot out at short notice, I can let you know and see if you are available...just in case.

Aaron

~~~~~~

A,

Yes, sure.

G

~~~~~~

G,

Great!!!

A

~~~~~~~

A,

XXXXXOOOOO

G

~~~~~~

G,

I would love those in reality. I told you the last time too I love sucking your tongue and when you do it too. I enjoyed that so much... and you?

A

~~~~~~

A,

And I replied that I did too and that I can't wait to be in your arms again.

You?

G

~~~~~~

Me too, Giuliana, and more.

A

~~~~~~

A,

Wow, great!

G

~~~~~~

G,

Would you like more too? Tell me what you like most during sex? I hope you do not mind me being free with our conversations?

Aaron

~~~~~~

A,

Wow, good question? I'm not answering for two reasons:

1]   I'm working.

2]   You'll have to figure that out on your own [isn't that the point?]

Ciao

Giuliana

~~~~~~~

G,

Good answer.

A

~~~~~~

A,

Thanks.

G

~~~~~~

G,

Welcome.

A

~~~~~~

A,

You know...last night I was reading the short stories you wrote to me on The Chat Net that night...and I was reminded why I started this whole thing.

G

~~~~~~

G,

Well, I am glad I left an indelible mark! :)

A

~~~~~~

A,

You sure did!

G

~~~~~~

G,

I look forward to keeping the next mark now!

A

~~~~~~

A,

We'll see.

G

~~~~~~

G,

Would you like me to?

A

~~~~~~

A,

Let's keep it a mystery, shall we?

138

G

Good morning, Sunshine!

How's your day going? I'm very busy but happy!

Ciao

Giuliana

~~~~~~

Morning Giuliana,

I was in very early today. I have a lunch meeting at 12.30pm and then some internal meetings for discussions about the purpose of our visit to that convention in Chicago. Tomorrow, I am out in London with another important client, which will take me all day long. So, you can see what a rat race this is!

Take care,

Aaron

~~~~~~

Hi,

Trust mA, I know well what a rat race your life is! If I didn't have all the patience I have, I would have given up on you by now.

So, are there any chances of meeting tonight?

Let me know.

Ciao

Giuliana

~~~~~~

Giuliana,

Let me see what transpires and I will let you know.

Okay?

~~~~~~

Aaron,

Okay.

G

~~~~~~

At the end of the workday, Giuliana turned her cell phone on as she left the office building. She noticed a message waiting. She picked up her message and it was Aaron. He said that he was on his way to the coffee shop they met on their second encounter. She left her cell on as she got into her car and made her way to the coffee shop.

She walked in, went to the counter and ordered a bottle of water, paid and went to a comfy chair and sat down. As she was waiting, her mind wandered. She thought of how the night was going to develop itself, what he organized, what he had in mind, what...her phone rang. She jumped in her chair, flipped open the phone. It was Aaron, he was coming, just a few more minutes. Was she as impatient as he was?

"Yes, I am. Stop yapping and hurry!"

"Ok, Sweetie." He grinned.

A few minutes later, he parked his Lexus in front of the coffee shop, right next to Giuliana's car. Her heart skipped a beat as he entered the coffee shop and saw her sitting there with her legs crossed.

Boy, she looked so sexy. He went up to her and kissed her lightly on her soft lips.

"So, what will you have Sweetie?"

"You know what I want, Aaron." She said as she pouted just a bit.

"Ah, yes, Espresso, right?" he said as he caressed her face.

"Right!" she gently caressed his face with her hand.

He felt tingling in his trousers when she did that.

A few minutes later he came back with her espresso and an iced tea for himself and placed them on the little table set between them.

"Boy, you look great, Sweetie! Can I kiss you again?" he said as he got up and headed towards her.

She blushed as she said: "Sure!"

It wasn't a light kiss this time but a very sensual and sodden kiss that sent a very clear message to Giuliana.

As Aaron sat back down again, he was licking his lips and said:

"Mmmmm that was sweet!"

"I know, I know" she said as she gave him that look.

"Ok, so we're going to the "Piatto D'Argento" for dinner and then I've booked a room for

later at the Hilton." He gave her the same look back.

"Sounds like a plan, babe!"

Aaron got up and took Giuliana's hand as she got up. They got into his Lexus and headed for the Restaurant. As the gentleman he always was, he opened the door for her, and she thanked him with a quick kiss on his cheek.

As they had dinner, they were talking about their families again. Aaron was updating her on his granddaughter, and she was telling him about her kids and what they were doing during the summer.

After they had dinner, Aaron ordered coffee and asked for the bill. While they were waiting for the waitress to come back Giuliana put her hand on Aaron's arm and whispered,

"Aaron, I want you to make love to me."

Aaron couldn't believe his ears! Did he hear what he just heard? Of course, it was their night tonight but never has any woman asked him straight out. Aaron placed his hand on hers as he squeezed it.

"It would be my pleasure." he whispered back.

He was impatiently tapping his fingers on the table as

the waitress came back with the receipt. Aaron got up and went up to Giuliana's chair and moved it back for her to get up, as she did, he kissed the side of her neck.

"Just a few more minutes, Sweetie."

Hand in hand, they quickly left the restaurant, and he opened the passenger door for her. Aaron quickly got in the car, turned it on and was headed for the Hilton. He was very excited, and it showed as he pounded his fists a couple of times on the steering wheel when they were caught in a bit of traffic.

CHAPTER ELEVEN

When his car was parked in the hotel parking lot, he let Giuliana out and put his arm around her shoulder as if to say to her that he would never leave her. They entered the hotel lobby; he went up to the desk and asked for the key to the room he had reserved. Before he turned around to signal Giuliana to follow him, he whispered something to the hotel director.

In the elevator, Aaron kissed Giuliana again, this time with deep passion and anticipation, without saying a word.

"So, what did you say to the director?" she asked as she gently touched his cheek.

"You'll find out soon enough, Sweetie." He responded as they headed towards their room.

Aaron opened the door and guided her in. She headed to the window to see the view.

"Look at the airport. I love the idea of coming and going, it's so exciting."

The light knocking on the door made Giuliana turn away from the window. A waiter came in with a bottle of champagne in an ice bucket and two flutes.

"It can also get boring at times too, especially when you have to travel for work. Going to a strange city, meeting strange people...sometimes I wish I had a nine to five job just like you."

"Isn't that funny, I would love to do what you do, and you wish you had my job. We're just never happy, are we?" she said as she took the glass of champagne that Aaron offered to her.

They clicked glasses and took a quick sip. He took both glasses, placed them on the coffee table. He took both her hands and kissed them. It made her tingle all over when he kissed her hands.

"So, tell me Sweetie, what were you saying back at the restaurant?"

"I said that I want you to make love to mA, Aaron." She said as she began to loosen his tie, unbutton his jacket and let it fall to his feet.

She started to kiss his neck as she unbuttoned his shirt.

He let her pull him with his tie towards the bed as she slipped the tie from his collar and threw it behind her shoulders. She began to unbutton one sleeve and then the other. His shirt fell on the floor as she gently moved her hands up and down his hairy chest while her warm lips were slowly discovering erotic spots all over his head and neck. With her hands on his shoulders, she turned him around as she turned with him and sat on the bed. Her hands slid down to unbutton his pants and slowly unzip his zipper.

"Oh, Baby! You're really something!" he whispered softly in her ear as he freed himself from his pants to show her how aroused he was.

He couldn't remember the provocation of the feelings and sensations that any woman was ever able to do to him. Suddenly, he remembered that she was still dressed. He got down to his knees, unbuckled her sandals, one by one and began kissing her feet while slowly sliding his hands up to her dress. As they were making their way upwards, he took hold of her dress and pulled it over the top of her head. He backed away from her to get a better look at her. She was wearing matching panties and bra in French black lace.

"Is something wrong?" she asked as she looked a bit puzzled.

"You're so beautiful, you know? And so sexy too! You make me want to explode! I can't wait anymore." He raised the tone of his voice when he said that.

"Then don't, Aaron, I'm all yours!" She opened her arms for him as she answered in a whisper.

"Oh, Sweetie, I …" he mumbled something as he pressed his lips on hers with frenzy, his tongue searching for hers, amalgamating to become one.

As he unhooked her bra, his hands, lips, and tongue were all over them as if they belonged only to him.

"Oh God! Aaron…" she groaned as she ran her fingers through his hair, tugging with pleasure.

Slowly, Aaron's hands made their way to her panties. Firmly, he grabbed them and slid them all the way down to her ankles. As he came back up again, he parted her knees and dug his tongue into her moist, warm, female lips. His tongue went up and down in search of that critical point he knew would fill Giuliana with ecstasy.

Giuliana was lying on her elbows, clinching the covers, she arched her back up and down, moaning and grunting with pleasure as Aaron was furiously sucking and teasing her clitoris. She reached her first orgasm with force and elation.

Aaron took hold of her by the waist and moved her towards the center of the bed as he also climbed on it. Once again, he parted her legs and penetrated her with rambling passion. At first, his movements were rapid and deep, then he slowed his pace to a regular thrust.

"I love you, Giuliana! My God, how I love you!"

He said to her as he was enjoying the look of pleasure she had on her face and the sounds of zeal coming out of her mouth. Finally, Aaron reached orgasm to climax an act of love that he never knew could be so fulfilling and out poured.

He was resting on her side for a moment when he noticed that she turned on her back to him. He heard faint sighing sounds as if she was…crying.

"Giuliana are you crying?" he asked her as he turned her so she was facing him. "Tell me, what's wrong? Did I do something you didn't like? What is it?"

"No, you were wonderful, Aaron, really. It's just that I'm afraid that now that we've made love, you're going to leave me and go back to your wife and…" her words were stifled by her crying.

"Oh, no, Sweetie, no. I could never do that to you! Didn't you hear what I said before, I love you, Giuliana" he turned her face so she could look into his eyes, "Listen to me. You're a part of me now and I will not give you up!"

Aaron wiped her tears and hugged her tightly. To think that she was crying for him made his feelings for her even deeper. Even if he still couldn't believe the words that came out of his mouth, he had no intention of letting her down and he could never leave her, never.

"I'm sorry, Aaron." She said as she was in his embrace. "I love you too, very much and that's why this fear came over mA, fear that you would consider me a one-night stand and after you would have gone back to your normal life. The last time I fell in love like this was with my husband!" she said still in his embrace.

"Well, let me tell you something, Giuliana;" He said as he took her face in his hands, "I've never been in love like this, not even with my wife. This is not a one-night stand, now that we've made love, I'll never leave you again, I promise." He sealed what he said to her with a kiss.

"What did you do to mA, Aaron? I've fallen for you so badly; you must have put some kind of spell on me." she said as she wiped her tears away from her face.

Aaron began to kiss her neck as he said:

"Well..." he kissed her chin, "You know..." he kissed her cheek, "I'm a..." he kissed her other cheek, "a magician." He kissed her lips with ardor as his hands were once again discovering her full and fleshy body.

"Ah, Aaron..."

He proceeded to kiss her all over and slowly made his

way to her forbidden area. Gently, he pulled apart her legs and began to work on her clitoris using his tongue. While working it gently and tenderly at the same time, he slightly blew on it made her shudder with ecstasy.

"My God! Aaron!" She yelled.

The more she yelled the more he worked until she couldn't take it any longer and roughly pushed his head away. He licked his lips and promptly moved towards her nipples. He proceeded to work them in the same manner again, making her tremble and quiver with pleasure.

About an hour later, they were lying in each other's arms, exhausted and not willing to get up. Giuliana got up first and headed for the shower.

"Someone has to start getting washed up!" She turned and gave him an inviting look, "Would you like to join me?"

"Would I!" He quickly got up and joined her in the shower.

Another hour later and they were dressed and ready to go. Aaron drove Giuliana to her car, and she went home.

As she was driving home, she noticed the time. 12:30 it wasn't that late, but she hadn't been home since morning. Her mind began to make up all the possible excuses for Rocco, but she knew that he wouldn't want to hear them, he trusted her. A terrible feeling of guilt and shame came over her so she starting crying.

"What have I done!" she yelled out loud. "My God! I still love Rocco, but I also love Aaron now. Is it possible to love two men at the same time?"

She had to pull over to the side of the road because she couldn't see due to the tears in her eyes. She laid her head on the steering wheel and wept frantically.

When she finally got home, she washed her face and went straight to bed. Rocco was fast asleep, of course. Giuliana kissed him on his forehead and whispered:

"Good night."

Then she turned to her side and quietly sobbed to sleep.

It was one morning when Aaron walked in the door. He was so in high spirits that he wanted to shout it to the four winds, but he was silent as a mouse. He took his shoes off, went upstairs, undressed and went to bed. Vivian was sleeping so he just kissed her on the cheek, lay on his back and looked at the ceiling. What a night! What a woman Giuliana was! What was he doing? Was he going through a mid-life crisis? He was a grandfather, for God's sake! Would this guilty feeling he had go away or would it devour his liver? He's never let his family down with something like this. What would they think of him? Questions, questions and more questions. He wasn't sure of anything anymore. One thing he was sure of though, he loved Giuliana, so much so that he desired her again. He tossed and turned all night long.

CHAPTER TWELVE

He noticed there was no email from his beloved
Giuliana in his inbox. Aaron began to panic. Then his cell
phone went off.

"Could it be?" he asked and sure enough, there was a
text message from her. He was relieved.

Good morning, Aaron!

I hope you don't mind my texting.

How did you sleep?

Ciao

> *Morning to you, Sweetie!*
>
> *At this point, texting is okay but
> please delete them, okay?*
>
> *I wanted you again last night, so I
> didn't sleep very well.*
>
> *What about you?*

Wow! He desired her again. She was so thrilled.

Aaron,

I didn't sleep well, either. I had all these mixed

feelings about what we did, about what I did

and all the guilt. It tormented me the whole night!

I'm sorry. That's probably not what you wanted to hear.

It was true. He wanted to hear that she enjoyed the evening and being with him. He wouldn't dare tell her that he had also felt the same way.

You're right, I don't want to hear that. But tell me honestly, did you enjoy our evening?

Oh yes! I did, really. Making love to you

was so wonderful and I wanted you again and again!

He was relieved. He also wanted her, and he wanted her right now.

Now that's what I want to hear! Thank you, Sweetie. You know that I'm aroused right now.

So was she.

We've got to stop this! We're both working and

there's no way of satisfying our desires. Right?

Why don't we change the subject?

He didn't want to change the subject! He wanted her, now!

You're absolutely right! We
to be rational about this.

Ok, Sweetie, what do you
want to talk about?

She was pleased that she was able to calm him down. Now, she had to try and change the subject.

Good boy! So, tell me,

how is your day going?

The rest of the day went pretty smoothly for Aaron. Even if she managed not to talk about that evening in their emails, he tried to go along with it as best as he could. By the end of the day he wasn't thinking about it at all but as soon as he got into his car, he called her cell.

"Hello." She answered.

"Giuliana, it's me. Can you talk?" he asked.

"Not right now. Can I call you back in a few minutes?" she was almost whispering.

"Ok, Sweetie." He answered as he pressed the end

button. He waited impatiently for her call as he slowly made his way home. Ten minutes had passed when his cell rang but to him it seemed an hour.

"Hello."

"Didn't you have enough of me today?" she asked in her sexiest voice.

"No, I didn't, Giuliana. I wanted you more today than any other day! At this moment, emails are not enough for me, I need to hear your voice, touch your skin…My God, Giuliana, what have you done to me? I feel like a teenager that has a crush on his teacher!" He raised the tone of his voice with that last comment.

"Aaron, you have no idea of what I'm going through! I have mixed feelings too, about Rocco, you, my kids and my life in general…but one thing I am sure about is loving you, Aaron, I do, so much. But I still love Rocco too, he's been in my life for such a long time, he totally trusts me, and I can't let him down. And my kids, they're part of me! I could never hurt them, never…" her voice was choked by the lump in her throat and her eyes were slowly filling with tears.

"Believe me, I have the same feelings. I've been with Vivian almost all my life and I can't let her down. Both my sons look up to me, I've always been their role model. And what about little Virginia...I'm her grandfather!" he swallowed the lump in his throat and continued "We have to be rational about this situation, but I want you so much that it's impossible!" He was hoping she was more rational than him.

"My God, Aaron, so do I, believe me! But I just can't leave and come to you now, I've got dinner and my usual routine. We were together just last night, and I can't go out every night. Rocco will really start to get suspicious." She looked over her shoulders to see if anyone was there.

"Really? You're absolutely right, we must be careful, or we'll end up being sorry." He felt his stomach turn as he said that.

"Well, then why don't we make a pact so we can avoid that?"

"Anything you want, Sweetie!" he said.

"Ok, let's agree to see each other once a week or whenever we have the chance. This way we won't put our families in jeopardy. How does that sound, Aaron?" It was all she could think of at that moment.

"It sounds good." He frowned a bit, "Although it doesn't stop me from wanting you, but I guess I have no choice." He was so aroused that he thought he was going to come right there and then!

"Right, we have no choice. We don't want anyone to get hurt, right? Please, Aaron, try to understand, it's hard for me to try and be rational one, but someone has to do it! When you get home, take a cold shower." She said that with a chuckle.

"Ha, ha…yes, as soon as I get home. Ok, Sweetie, we'll chat tomorrow then. Love you." She did it, she tranquillized him.

"I love you too, Aaron. Till tomorrow. Bye." She said as she pressed the end button. He was calm now and she felt much better as well.

She went back to making dinner and went on with her

evening as usual. Later on, she went for her usual walk with her daughter. Anastasia went on talking and talking about her friends and what she did during the day, but Giuliana couldn't stop thinking about Aaron. She was very in love with this man. Just the thought of their evening of passion made her spine tingle. He possessed everything that Rocco didn't. He was romantic, wise, kind, intelligent and passionate. Rocco was a good husband and a good father, but he definitely lacked romance, wisdom and intelligence. Giuliana was always the romantic one because she thought that most of men were not romantic. Boy, was she wrong. She was always the smarter one as he wasn't the brightest tool in the shed. Aaron was everything she needed in her life right now and all she really wanted was to be with him night and day. On the other hand, she didn't want to lose Rocco or her family. She got a chill just thinking of what would happen if they were to find out about Aaron. She had to be very careful of her children, especially since she didn't have the courage to disappoint them. She was torn between her Aaron and her family.

As soon as Aaron walked in the door, he headed straight for the shower and as he promised Giuliana, took a cold one. His thoughts were for Giuliana and the power she had over him already. He was amazed at her ability to calm him and excite him at the same time. He had never had this type of relationship with a woman, not even Vivian. He never had these feelings for her, of desire, passion and romance. With Vivian it was just doing his Christian duty. Gilda was much different. When they first met, desire was there, and it was an affair. Plain and simple. Romance had always been his way of life with both of them, but he certainly never remembered or experienced this kind of passion. Until now.

CHAPTER THIRTEEN

Good morning, Aaron.

How are things today?

> *Good morning to you*
> *Giuliana,*
>
> *Much better than last night.*
> *How about you, Sweetie?*

Aaron looked forward to her texts and couldn't wait for them to arrive. He was feeling better. To fill his evening with excitement, he went to visit his granddaughter. It was amazing how much life there is in such a small human being.

Hi Aaron,

I'm all right. My evening went by in the usual way,

dinner, walk with my kids and of course,

thinking about you. What did you do?

He was now in her thoughts all the time lately.

> *I went to visit my precious*
> *Victoria. I'm telling you that*
> *little girl is something else.*
> *She's really similar to you,*

you know, Giuliana. Both of
you have the power to make
me forget my troubles.

It gives me joy to know that
you're thinking about me.
Same here.

She was always on his mind as well lately. The phone
rang and it was Vivian. She just wanted to know what he was
doing and when he was coming home. This seemed very odd to
him as she was never really interested in what he was doing at
work. Why was she starting now? Maybe she was suspicious.
Was he so transparent? Did she notice that he was different?

I know, Aaron, especially since we've made love,
you're always been on my mind.

You're my first thought when I wake up in
the morning and you're my last thought when
I fall asleep at night. But I still have my life
to live, I've got three kids to take care of
and I have Rocco as well, who I don't want
to leave because I still love him. It's a love

164

that has always been there for me, do you

understand, Aaron?

She couldn't just leave her husband, he didn't deserve it at all, and he was rough on the edges but still remained a good man.

Yes, I do understand, Giuliana. I too, have a special relationship with Vivian and I could never leave her. And I couldn't do that to my family. I have never let the family down and I think my guilt will eat me up alive!

This was something he could never do, just the thought of it was making his stomach turn. Giuliana, though, was different from the others he had in his past or maybe it was that she entered into it this particular time of his life.

See, so we both agree. We don't want to ruin

our families and both love each other

and we both want to be together so why

don't we just keep things as they are.

We'll see each other whenever we can.

What do you think, Aaron?'

This was the best solution she could come up with right now. It was a very practical solution even though he wanted to be with her every day, however considering their family situations he had to accept it.

I think it's a good idea,

though I would have preferred

being with you every day. But

you're absolutely right, we

don't have the right to hurt

our families because of our

selfishness. We have to be

objective so yes, let's do it this

way for now.

166

What do you mean, for now?

This is not a temporary solution,

Aaron, we must keep our

relationship realistic, please?

He was being a bit stubborn but the two could play that game.

> *You're a tough lady, you*
> *know that! But I love you anyway* ☺

I know I am and I love you too

Here's a kiss to seal our pact.

A kiss emoji appeared.

> *Right back at you, Sweetie!*

At least she had her head screwed on the right way. Practicality was not typical of many women, but she had plenty of it. Giuliana was surprising Aaron day by day by showing these new sides of her personality. She could be so passionate and audacious and at the same time reserved and conservative.

Aaron's day proceeded with a quick lunch and general

management meeting in the afternoon. At 5:30 he left. After half an hour of rush hour traffic he got home, changed his clothes and made himself a quick sandwich.

As it was Friday and it was a beautiful July afternoon, he decided to go for a round of golf. During the summer season, he keeps his clubs in the truck of the Lexus, so he is ready anytime he decides to attack the greens. He was an avid golfer. Whenever he needed to relax and unwind, this sport would do it for him. He found himself particularly tense during the last couple of months mainly because of his situation with Giuliana. He definitely didn't regret meeting Giuliana and getting himself involved with her, but his life was tumultuous right now because of her. His feelings for her were conflicting with him being a family man. Sometimes he wondered what was going to happen next and this created tension, tension that he was able to suppress with his favorite pastime, golf.

Giuliana was very satisfied as the end of the workday and workweek drew to a close. Naturally, she was well aware that her weekends could never be spent with Aaron. As she walked out the door, she noticed that there wasn't a cloud in the sky, and this meant that Aaron would have spent this weekend on the golf course. She didn't like golf at all, she found it very boring, but Aaron was an executive and like most people in his rank, they loved to golf. He was no exception. She respected his private, everyday life and he respected hers. She would never become a threat to him in any way and she was very happy to be with him whenever he had a chance.

She was amazed by the latest events in her life. Up until a few months ago, she would never have considered having another man in her life. She had always been of sound principals, especially when it came to her family. She went to church every Sunday and spent all the time she could with her children. Lately, though, there was something missing in her life and Aaron found it for her. He was romantic, charming and honest. She loved the romantic versus she wrote to her, the romantic things he said to her, the compliments he filled her with, the way he called her "Sweetie", the way he touched her and especially the way he loves her.

Even though it went against all her deep beliefs, she had to admit to herself that her life was complete at this point in time. She was thankful that Aaron was in her life and that he was the way he was, a very busy free spirit.

Samuele was working the closing shift at Burger King on Saturday and Giuliana had to pick him up because he hadn't driven yet. She decided to wait for his call while online. She was catching up with her chat buddies and she decided to click on Aaron's profile. She smiled when she saw his introductory line again:

"Gentle, kind businessman, looking for clean chat, love to travel, avid golfer and free spirit."

Then she clicked the personal information tab and noticed that his birthday was July 28 which was only a week away! She started thinking of what she could buy for him. She didn't want to get him anything big, but it had to be something that reminded him of her. A tie. He was a businessman, he always wore one, for sure. A red tie. Red was her favorite color, and it was also the color for passion and love, exactly like their love. Her decision was made.

The next day she went to the mall to begin her search. She searched every menswear department of the major department stores. Nothing. She searched every man's store in the mall. Nothing. Although there were many red ties but none of them had grasped her attention. She decided to go to the greeting card store and look for a birthday card. She decided to send him the card first and maybe she could have given him the tie when they met again. Just thinking about that future encounter gave her chills up and down her spine.

Which card to pick? That was the question. Cards that said "Happy Birthday to my secret lover" didn't exist. She noticed many cards for lovers, boyfriends, fiancés and husbands, but which one. She noticed a card that had a very romantic poem written on the front cover and another poem written inside, but she thought that it was too much poetry for Aaron. She concluded that he didn't need poetry, he wrote beautiful poetry. Then she noticed a very simple card that said "The thing I love about us......" on the front cover and on the inside, it continued "is you. Happy Birthday my love!" Very simple, very sweet and it got the message across. Sold. At the counter, they gave her a wind-up butterfly made of colorful paper that flew out when you opened the card. She loved it and she thought it would be fascinating for his granddaughter.

On Monday morning, she brought the card with her to work so she could send it from there. She simply signed it "Giuliana", she dabbed a few drops of her perfume on it, wound up the butterfly, carefully placed it inside the card, closed it and inserted it into the envelope. On the envelope she wrote the address and "Private and Confidential", put the stamp on and placed it in her out basket.

Like every Monday morning, she sent Aaron an email.

Good morning, Aaron?

How was your weekend?

Love

Giuliana

~~~~~

Good morning to you Giuliana. My weekend was great! Lots of golfing…ha ha…I know you hate golf. ☺ *What did you do, Sweetie?*

Aaron

~~~~~~

Yes, I do. Oh well, we can't agree on everything right. I had a good weekend, too, lots of shopping…ha ha…I know you hate shopping…like all men.

So, what's your week looking like? I really want you.

Giuliana

~~~~~~

Yes, right again. I'm leaving for Cleveland tomorrow and I should be back Thursday night. Maybe we can meet on Friday? What do you think, Sweetie? Even for a short while? Lord knows, I want you terribly!

XXOO

Aaron

~~~~~~

Yes, of course we can. Friday is so far away but I think I can handle four days. Even if you hold me for ten minutes, I'll be happy.

Love

Giuliana

~~~~~~

You're the best, Giuliana. I will let you know as soon as I get back, Okay?

Love you,

Aaron

~~~~~~

I'll be here, Aaron, and waiting.

Love you too,

Giuliana

The day continued with the coming and going of their emails. Giuliana loved texting with him while she was busy at work. They wrote about many things, their respective families, business and their relationship. She loved hearing that musical notification when his texts arrived because it was, most of the time, a reply from her Aaron.

At the end of his workday Aaron left the office and headed for home. As he drove into the driveway, he noticed his wife sitting in one of the wicker chairs on the porch. He also noticed that something was wrong because her face clearly showed her foul mood.

"Hello, Vivian, how was your day?" He tried to say it cheerfully.

"Do you really care, Aaron? Do you care about me at all?" she asked with a chilling tone.

"Of course I do, Viv, you're my wife, aren't you?" He answered but he didn't like where this was going.

"Yes, I am. Unfortunately!" She yelled.

"Ok. Why don't we go inside?" Aaron asked as he was looking around for curious neighbors. He opened the door for her.

"I really don't care about the neighbors!" She yelled as she went inside. "I want them to hear what kind of man you are!"

Aaron quickly closed the door.

"And what kind of man would I be?" He asked her very calmly.

"Not one who acts his age, that's for sure! You should be ashamed of yourself, doing these things at your age!" She raised her voice even more.

"Vivian, please tell me what's going on?" Aaron knew exactly what was going on. He was just trying to figure out how to handle it.

"I know, Aaron! I know about you and *THAT* woman!" She was yelling as she paced up and down the corridor. "How could you do this to me? Again! You promised last time that it would never happen again!" She covered her face with her hands, "You promised." She plopped down on the couch.

Aaron saw the tears and his stomach was turning. "You're right, I did promise and I'm sorry, really. I didn't mean to hurt you again. But how did you find out?" He sat down beside her.

"Olga! She's been keeping an eye on you, and she's copied some of your disgusting emails and sent them to me! I keep them in a safe place, and I won't hesitate to use them against you, Aaron!" When she felt his hand on her arm, she immediately got up and went into the kitchen. She was fuming.

"God dammit, Olga! I can't believe this! And after I've helped her out with her second mortgage, this is the thanks I get!" The tone of his voice was in disbelief. He slowly sat in a chair at the kitchen table. "Ok, so what do you want me to do? I'll admit it, I'm having an affair with her. How do you plan on using those emails?" Although he was terrified, he looked her straight in the eyes.

"For starters, I'll show your sons what type of father and grandfather you are! Then, I'll show them to the lawyer. I'm pretty sure I can get a good settlement with all this evidence and don't forget that I still have the pictures from you previous romance!" She yelled in the most awful way as she sat in a chair right across from him.

"No! Don't do this to me, Viv, I couldn't bear it! You

know me very well, I never let those boys down and I never will!" His tone was desperate, and his hands started to shake. Then he tried to put a smile on his face and asked, "Tell me what I have to do to avoid this, please?" He raised himself from his chair to reach over to her hand and held it in his.

"You've disappointed me, that's for sure, but I don't want our sons to suffer because of your sexual cravings. Just think that you're a grandfather! This should calm your urges, but I see very clearly that it doesn't!" The tone of her voice was slowly lowering, and she kept her hand in his. "I still love you, Aaron, despite everything. I know you're also very ambitious and I don't want to ruin your career." She let go of his hand and stood up, "therefore you will leave her immediately! No more emails, no more phone calls, no more text messages and especially no more meetings! Clear?" She ordered loud and clear.

"C...Clear." He barely whispered it as he had a lump in his throat.

Vivian got up and went upstairs. He crossed his arms

on the table and laid his head on them. "God, how am I going to tell Giuliana!" he cried out. He couldn't leave her! He was in love with her Damn it! And Damn Olga! What a bitch she turned out to be! He couldn't even fire her because this is not a valid reason as it doesn't affect the company. Damn! He slowly got up and went upstairs to pack for his trip.

CHAPTER FOURTEEN

When Aaron opened up his inbox, he noticed that the first email on his list was from Giuliana.

Good morning, Aaron,

Are you back?

XXOO

Giuliana

This was so hard for him. What should he do? Naturally, she wanted to see him, and he definitely wanted to see her and kiss her and hold her and......

Morning Giuliana,

Yes, I am.

Aaron

~~~~~~

Good, I'm so happy. How did it go?

XXOO

Giuliana

~~~~~~

He loved her emails. She was such a thoughtful and caring person. He just couldn't bear to hurt her.

The receptionist popped in to deliver his mail. He immediately noticed a different colored envelope and concluded that it was a greeting card. He took his letter opener and opened it. It was from Giuliana because her perfume filled his lungs like smoke from a much-desired cigarette. He pulled it out and read the front cover.

"The thing I love about us......" When he opened it, a butterfly came flying out, swirled up in the air and landed on the floor. He looked stunned when he picked it up and placed it inside the card again. He read the inside. "is you. Happy Birthday my love!" Short and sweet. It was typical of Giuliana and that's what he loved about her the most, her simplicity. He took another whiff of her perfume, put the card back in its envelope and locked it up in his secret drawer. He went back to his email.

Very well. Contacted many new clients for a new pharmaceutical line that we're launching.

I just received your card, Giuliana, thanks. You have no idea how much I appreciate this, and I won't forget it.

XXOO

Aaron

~~~~~~

You're welcome. I'm glad you liked it. You could give the butterfly to your granddaughter, I'm sure she'll love it.

So, tell mA, did you miss me?

XXOO

Giuliana

God, yes! His desire for her was pounding right now.

Of course I did. Would you be able to meet tonight?

Aaron

~~~~~~

Yes, I've been waiting all week, Aaron. I've missed you so. Just tell me where and when.

Ciao

Giuliana

Screw his wife. He thought it was the best thing to do. He had to meet her so he could tell her what was going on but he didn't know if he would be able to look her in the eye and tell her it was over.

Great! We'll meet in our usual place, okay. Keep your cell on just in case I'm late. Let's say around 5?

Aaron

~~~~~~

Sounds good. I can't wait!

I love you.

Giuliana

~~~~~~

So do I, baby, so do I.

Aaron

~~~~~~

Finally, 4:30 came and Giuliana was on her way to that mall in Brampton. Strangely enough, she never actually shopped in that mall because her favorite mall was Square One. She was thinking of visiting it this time around. She was immersed in her thoughts when her cell phone rang, the display showed "Aaron Cell".

"Hey, you!" She said joyfully.

"Hi Sweetie. How are you?" He tried to sound happy.

"Great! Where are you?"

"I've just left the office. I think I might get there around 5:30. Is that ok, Sweetie?"

"Of course. I'll just do a bit of shopping while to kill time."

"You women and shopping! Ok, see you then. Love you, baby!"

"I love you too. Bye Babe."

She arrived at the mall around five, so she decided to go inside the mall and take a look around. Maybe she could find a suitable tie for Aaron. As soon as she walked in, she noticed a second cup kiosk, so she decided to have an espresso. She really enjoyed her espresso after work because it relaxed her.

With her espresso in hand, she began her browsing. She decided not to enter the larger department stores as she already knew that they probably wouldn't have what she was looking for.

She noticed a store called "Men's Imports". As she entered, a young clerk acknowledged her with a smile. He was very handsome, and he looked like he was East Asian. She imagined that Aaron would have probably looked like him when he was younger. She smiled back and he immediately headed her way.

"Hello, there. How are you today?" He asked her while he showed her his straight set of teeth.

"Fine, thanks." She smiled as she handed him her empty cup. "Where can I throw this out?"

"Oh, don't worry. I'll throw it for you." He quickly took the cup and headed behind the cash counter. He was back in a split second. "Is there anything else I could do for you?"

She looked him in the eyes, they were very captivating.

"I'm looking for a tie for a gift."

The clerk turned and showed Giuliana to another corner of the store.

"This way, please. Anything in particular?" He asked.

"Red and silk, if possible."

"Ah red, color of passion. Yes, we have some available. Here, take a look." He picked up a few red ties and distributed them on the table.

For a split second, Giuliana's mind flashed back to a moment of passion in that hotel room, and she felt a tingle in her lower abdomen.

"What do you think about this one?" He asked.

She came back to reality and looked at the tie. It was red with half circles going up and down. She picked it up and turned it around, it was 100% silk, by Gucci. Sold.

"Oh, I love it. I'll take it. Could you gift wrap it for me?"

"Of course! It will take a minute. Please follow me." In a few minutes it was neatly wrapped and paid for.

Giuliana looked at her watch, at almost 5:30, so she headed for the entrance. As she came out, she scanned the parking lot and saw his Lexus.

Aaron saw her at the main entrance. His stomach tightened. She looked radiant, happy and so sexy. He pulled over as she opened the door and sat herself in the seat.

"Hi, Baby! Boy, you look great!" He said as he kissed

her. "And you smell great too!" He said as he took a whiff of her perfume.

"Mmmm, and you kiss great! So, how are you, Babe?" She asked him as he made his way to a dark spot in the lower level of the parking lot.

"Oh, I'm stressed out. Work is crazy, home is crazy, and my sugar level is very high these days." He sighed as he parked the car.

"You have diabetes? I didn't know that." She said as she caressed his face, but she suddenly got a gut feeling that something was wrong.

"God! I've missed you, Aaron!" She threw her arms around him and kissed his neck.

"Come on, let's go in the back seat." She opened her door and hopped into the back seat as Aaron did the same.

"Oh, that's much better. Isn't it?"

"Yes, come here, baby!"

He demanded as he pulled her towards him. He pressed his lips against her so he could show her how he missed her and his burning desire for her. Slowly, he kissed his way under her chin and on her chest while one of his hands was unhooking her bra and the other was lifting her shirt to free her breasts from the bra. He gently licked her nipples and delicately bit them.

"Uhhhh." She groaned at such skill, and she thought that she was going to lose it right there. She began to run her fingers through her hair while kissing and blowing gently in his ear.

"Am I relieving your stress, Aaron?" She whispered.

"Mmmm, yes Baby." He moaned as he moved her, so she was on her back now. He moved down and laid his head to rest on her cozy belly.

"So, what's going on at home and work? Do you want to talk about it?" She asked him as she gently massaged the back of his neck.

No, he didn't want to talk about it, but he had to at this point.

"Well, it's not a great moment at work at all. I have so

much traveling to do but what I really need is a vacation. Then, there's my wife, she's driving me up the wall." He straightened himself up.

"Why?" She asked.

"She must have suspicions about us. She's threatening to tell my sons and go to the lawyer!" He raised his voice and anger was written all over his face. "Don't get me wrong, I still love her, she's a great lady but lately she's pressuring me. She's continuously asking where I'm going, how long I'll be there and why I am going there. I'm starting to get fed up." He said as he laid his head on her belly again.

"Oh God! What will you do, Aaron?" she said as she began slowly massaging his neck. That gut feeling came back again.

"Nothing really. I've decided to lay low for a while or until the storm is over. She's using my sons as a weapon against me, and I can't risk letting them down." He said as he got up and took her in his arms. "But I do love you and I can't let you go either. Would you wait for me, Giuliana?" He began stroking her hair.

"You know I would do anything for you, and you also know that I don't want you to leave your family. I don't care how long I have to wait for you. Whatever time you want to dedicate to me is good. You want to lay low, fine, we will." She looked up so she could look him in the eyes. "I love you, Aaron, and I'll wait for you, no matter how long it takes. Ok?" She said as she ran her fingers through his hair.

Aaron felt a lump in his throat.

"You're the best! God, I'm so happy I have you, Giuliana!" He hugged her again, tighter this time as if he never wanted to part.

"Me too. I thank God every night that you came into my life. I know we're both Catholic and we shouldn't be doing this, but our love can't be a bad thing if we're both happy." Then she whispered in his ear. "So, where are we going for your birthday, Babe?" She slowly passed her tongue all over his ear and down his neck.

"Oh Baby!" He said as his hand was slowly moving his

hand up her leg as he hits the top of her thigh, then he moves it back down to her knee.

"A nice hotel room. Hummmm"

Back up her leg, a little higher this time, then down. Up and down, he goes, teasing her with his fingers, until he could feel her anticipation.

"Uhhh, yes, touch me, Aaron!"

She moans as she tightly grabs on to his shirt. Aaron slowly slid his hand inside her panties and began to massage her clitoris while kissing her on her neck. She was so hyped up that she couldn't hold it back any longer. She came with fervor and much moisture.

She opened her eyes for a moment, and she suddenly froze when she saw two kids peeking through the window.

"Aaron! Stop!"

She yelled as she pushed him away.

"Turn around!"

She giggled as Aaron turned to look at the two curious faces pressed against the window.

"Shew, shew!" He said to them as they took off. He turned to Giuliana who was still giggling and joined her.

"Ha, ha, I think we better stop now, ha ha, before the cops come and arrest us!" She was still laughing as she hooked up her bra and lowered her top and skirt.

"I hate to admit it, but you're right." He pressed his lips with fervor against hers. "Before we go, I've got to thank you again for the card."

She caressed his face and said:

"Don't mention it. Oh, just so you know, my birthday is on August thirty first. Okay?"

He closed his eyes for a moment and said:

"Saved it in my memory."

He laughed as he opened the door and climbed into the driver's seat.

"We'll see if you remember. Most husbands don't."

She said as she brought herself to the front seat as well.

"Well, I won't. Don't worry!" He reassured her as he winked.

"Okay, whatever you say."

She pulled out her handkerchief and started looking for spots of lipstick on Aaron's face and neck.

"If we're going to lay low then we'd better clean you up a bit."

She wet the tip of the handkerchief with her tongue and began to clean up the spots she noticed.

"Boy, you're reminding me of my mother. She used to clean my face in the same way. I used to hate it."

"And do you still hate it?" she asked as she kept cleaning.

"Not when you do it, Baby!" He grabbed her arm and kissed it, moving up and down.

"Stop it! Behave yourself and let me finish!" She yelled as she moved her arm briskly back to his face.

"Meanie!" He yelled back as he kissed her on her cheek. He started the car and brought her back to her car.

"Okay, Aaron, have a good weekend and I'll email you on Monday, Okay?" She said as she kissed him and caressed his face.

"Okay, Baby, love you." He said as he took her hand and kissed it.

"I love it when you do that, Ciao Babe!" She opened the door, and she was gone.

"I'll miss you."

He whispered so only he could hear. He stayed and watched her drive away. It would have been the last time that he would see her, and he knew it. But she didn't.

When he got home, he went straight upstairs as he didn't feel like facing his wife. But Vivian was already upstairs. She was putting some towels away in the linen closet. He didn't even look at her, he went straight in the bedroom and began to undress.

She followed him in. She was keeping a vigil eye on him since the talk they had. She picked up his golf shirt from the floor and immediately noticed that it smelled of perfume.

"Did you see her tonight?"

He stopped in his steps, but he didn't turn.

"Vivian, please, I'm not in the mood for arguing." He said as he continued towards the bathroom.

"You did, didn't you? This is unbelievable! Did you even hear a word I said to you the other day?" Her tone was very malicious. "That's it! Monday I'm going to the lawyer! How's that for a birthday present?" and she threw the shirt on the floor.

At those words, Aaron, came out of the bathroom.

"There's no need for that, Viv, I ended it. Okay! Are you happy now?" His face showed how miserable he was.

"Yes! Now *YOU* can feel the way I've been feeling for all these years!" She shouted as she left the room. She didn't speak to him for the rest of the weekend.

He didn't care. He preferred silence to her commands. He would rather think about his Giuliana for the rest of the weekend.

CHAPTER FIFTEEN

As soon as Giuliana turned on her computer on Monday morning, she clicked the internet on and sent Aaron an e-card. There, so now he would have two cards from her. She was satisfied now. She waited an hour before emailing him so he could get into his office, turn on his computer and read his emails. At 9:30 she emailed him.

Good morning and HAPPY BIRTHDAY!

Giuliana

After an hour, he finally replied.

Thanks Giuliana, I appreciate it. Just came into the office.

Aaron

~~~~~~

Did you get a big party last night? Is that why you're late?

Giuliana

Sure, some party. This must have been the worst weekend of his life.

Well, I had a meeting Downtown this morning... something I could not cancel. Thanks for your wishes and the e-card. I appreciate it.

Aaron

~~~~~~

My pleasure. So, no party last night?

Ciao

Giuliana

He had to break her heart today. His pain was so bad
that he just wanted to leave the office and never come back.

*No, but today everyone is coming to my son's place in Whitby and
going out for dinner... then, I do not have to drive back home and
return to Whitby again... so that's the plan.*

Aaron

~~~~~~

*Sounds great! You'll be with your granddaughter so I'm sure
you'll have a great time, eh Grandpa?*

Giuliana

Very true. At least he had his precious Victoria to help
him through this.

You bet! She is my pride and joy.

Aaron

Giuliana was getting a strange feeling, and she didn't know why.

I just wanted to thank you for Friday. You kept your promise and that means a lot to me...even if it was for a short while.

Ciao

Giuliana

His desire was to stay with Giuliana forever but...

Thanks for understanding. That's my life and I cannot see any changes in the near future. It's crazy but true Giuliana.

Aaron

Why was he telling her this, she knew it already. That gut feeling came back.

Aaron,

You know how I feel about you, and I've already told you that I'll wait for you. We've already agreed to lie low for a while. You also know that I understand your situation perfectly and that I wouldn't do anything to hurt you.

But now, you tell mA, is something wrong? Did something

happen during the weekend? My woman's intuition is acting up so

please be honest with me.

Giuliana

Never underestimate the power of a woman's intuition.

He had to tell her now, this was it.

Giuliana,

No absolutely nothing...just that it is so silent after Friday night,

that it is deafening...

You are a nice person Giuliana, and I do respect you as a Lady.

However, I feel that my life will never change and my dedication to

the family is too intense and whatever they do to mA, I will

always be the same husband and dad. So, you see Giuliana, I do

not want to lead you on in any way.

We will always be friends and I will really like this. Today being

another year in my life, I kissed my granddaughter and promised

her within my heart that I would never let them down any day. I

know you will say... but it's your life. However, G... I have never

let the family down and I think my guilt will eat me up alive...

Hope you understand my situation...

Aaron

Giuliana had to re-read the email and as she did her eyes were filling with tears. She couldn't believe it! This could not be happening. That gut feeling she had was dead on! Her hands were trembling as she replied to him.

Aaron,

I knew it. I felt it on Friday, Aaron. Your emails have not been the same either. I know your feeling of guilt very well because I've never done this either, never.

So, you want to end it then? Okay. Like I told you already, whatever makes you happy but there's one problem though, Aaron, I'm in love with you now. I'm trying so hard to hold my tears back, really. Silly mA, I even bought you a little present and I wanted to give it to you on a special occasion. But it's okay, I guess. I'll get over it.

Giuliana

"God! I love you too, Giuliana!" He yelled at his computer screen. How he wished he was there with her to hold her and tell her that everything was going to be all right.

Giuliana,

You see that I tried to avoid this so much. Right now, it's too much for mA, and with what's going on around me now and my family really doubting what I say...I cannot afford to fall in love with anyone.

I feel flattered you feel this way Giuliana, but I have to be honest with you and myself. I stopped going through with feelings long ago, and this is no exception Giuliana.

It's hard for me right now, and I hope my life will change for the better as I enter another year of my life.

That's why I told you that I will not want to lead you on in any way. I have to be honest and if I do not say this to you honestly then I will not be the gentleman that I feel I am.

Aaron

What the hell was he talking about! What's happened to him? He's flattered that she loves him! He can't afford to fall in love! He told her that he loved her so many times and now he's being honest! It felt like a bomb blowing up in her face. She was falling apart. She couldn't work anymore. She felt she had to throw up and she ran to the bathroom. After she was done throwing up, she stayed in the cell to cry out her tears, but she couldn't stop them. She came out of the cell, washed her face and went back to her desk. She tried to recompose herself as she didn't want anyone to notice the state she was in. She re-read his email again and once again her hands were shaking as she typed.

Aaron,

I do appreciate your honesty, really. You've always been honest, right from the start. I guess that's what attracted me to you, among the other things. Boy! Your wife must have really put some heavy spell or curse on you because you had such a sudden change of heart! I was so willing to take it slow with you, I just wanted you to be happy with me. I never wanted anything more, believe me. So, this is it. I would have preferred you to tell me in person but I guess this is the way it started and this is the way it has to end. But please, allow me to leave you with a little string of hope…if you ever change your mind, Aaron, you know where I am. I love you and I'll miss you so.

Giuliana

"Damn it!" He shouted again at the screen as he pounded his fist on his desk.

"Is everything ok?" His secretary asked as she peeked into his office.

"Yes!" He shouted back at her. God! How he wanted to take out his anger on her, but he held back with difficulty.

As Olga left him alone in his office, she smirked as she turned her back to him.

He took a deep breath and replied to Giuliana.

Giuliana,

Please do not make it harder for me than it is right now. I am under so much stress that you would never know. I do not want to get you into the mess I am in right now. It's too much, believe me.

I am sorry for making you sad, Giuliana, it was not the intention.

Thanks, and I will think of you as the Lady I knew but never knew…

Aaron

Giuliana couldn't believe what she was reading. "The Lady I knew but never knew..." What the hell was that! They made love, for God's sake! She broke out crying again and again she went to the ladies room to wash her face and let all her tears come out.

Aaron,

I'm sorry, I didn't mean to, but please try and understand what I'm going through. I say yes to a man met on chat and then I end up falling in love with him, it's crazy for me too. But you also still remain a friend, so if you ever feel you need to talk to someone, please do. I'll always be there for you, Aaron. You know I can make you feel better, even if it is through email or phone. I won't push you in any way, I promise. I've always left it up to you and I will this time too. If you ever do decide to meet me again, which I hope you will, I'll be here. I look forward to your emails, so you decide, okay. I'll respect any decision you make. Just let me give you a small piece of advice. Your life belongs to you and you alone, Aaron, not your wife, not your kids and not even your grandchildren. Don't give up a bit of selfish happiness for others.

You'll be able to do it for a month, a year but then you'll be

chatting again searching for someone new. I won't forget you either,

Aaron, not for a long time, that's for sure.

Ciao Giuliana

Aaron realized that she knew him better than himself.
He knew perfectly well that she was right. Every single word
she wrote was correct, but he couldn't tell her that right now.
He had to keep calm and finish what he started.

Thanks Giuliana and let me tell you that in my books you will

always be the Lady I met. You have so much class and you

deserve someone who can give you the same affection, because mine

would not be something you would expect.

I will never again be on chat, and certainly would never break a

heart again. It's too much and I do not have the heart to see this

happen. See what I have already done?

Thanks for being there for mA, and yes, once everything is sorted

out in my life, I will call you and let you know how I am and also

to find out how you are.

Till then Giuliana, it was great knowing a real Lady. I never thought I would meet someone like that through chat line. Your

hubby should be glad to have a person like you.

Take care, Aaron

After lunch, Giuliana returned to her desk. She couldn't eat much, and she certainly wasn't paying any attention to the usual conversation being held during lunch. She just couldn't stop thinking of Aaron. "What happened?" was the question she kept asking herself. Did his wife find out? How did she find out? Did she tell his sons? As she read his email, she realized that this was the last email she would be receiving from him. It was the last time that the little yellow envelope showed an email in her inbox. It took her a long time to click on her Inbox to read this last email. Finally, she did. As she read it, she felt her lunch coming back up. Just like going on a roller coaster ride right after eating. She ran to the ladies room again. When she was done, she looked at herself in the mirror. God! She was a mess! Her eyes were swollen, her face was pale, and her makeup was long gone. While still crying, she washed her face and tried to pat her eyes with cold water. She gave up and went back to her desk.

Thanks, Aaron, for your nice words. There will always be a corner of my heart for you, and don't you forget it. I'll still go on chat, but I won't fall in love with anyone else, that's for sure! I know I shouldn't be telling you this, but still dream of us being together again, in that hotel room, remember? And your wife, she doesn't deserve a man like you and she's much luckier than my husband. But it's okay. Like I said before I'll get over it, sooner or later. So, take care, Aaron and good luck to you.

One last XXXX Giuliana

As he finished reading her email, Aaron felt his desire for her growing. Why did he have to fall in love with her? He got what he wanted, sex. That's what it started as, only sex. He never would have imagined Giuliana being so thoughtful, caring, passionate and sexy. He concluded that it was the right thing to do, for both of them. He knew very well that she would never give up her family for him. In the same way she knew that his family was more important to him than his own life. She understood that and she communicated it loud and clear in her last email. Still, he wished he was with her to comfort her and hold her. His mind wandered to better times which were only a few weeks ago. He crossed his arms on his desk, laid down his head and closed his eyes. He was imagining how much Giuliana was hurting right now. She would get through it for sure because she was also strong and understanding.

He thought of her last sentence "One last XXXX". Her kisses, even if they were only X's on paper, he could taste her lips, feel their softness and the heat of their passion. He could still feel the softness of her skin when he kissed her neck and slowly moving down to her breast and…

"Aaron, are you okay?"

He immediately snapped back to reality as he popped his head up to see the president at his office door.

"We have a meeting, remember?" he asked as he headed for the boardroom.

"Coming, coming…" Reluctantly he got up and followed him to the boardroom.

CHAPTER SIXTEEN

Before Giuliana left the office for the day, she stopped in the ladies room one more time. She was officially a wreck. Her eyes were so swollen that she could barely see, and she also noticed a few new wrinkles that she never had until today.

"My God! What am I going to tell Rocco?" she asked herself out loud. She left the building and got into her car. She turned on her cell phone hoping for a phone call from Aaron. Nothing. Then she looked for a text message. Nothing. She slowly made her way home as tears kept running down her face. As she parked her car in the driveway, she dried her eyes one last time hoping that she wouldn't burst out crying in front of everyone. She would have had some explaining to do then.

When she walked in the kitchen, Rocco was preparing espresso coffee, as he usually did after work. He turned towards Giuliana to kiss her, as always.

"My God! Look at your eyes! You've been crying?" He asked her as he stared into her eyes.

She swallowed the knot in her throat and said, "No, I

woke up this way this morning. I've already been to the doctor, and she said that it's some kind of allergy but it's only a temporary thing."

"Oh, okay, if the doctor said so, fine. Did she give you anything for it?" he asked her as he gently touched her cheek.

"No, just patting them with cold water. Hopefully, it will last only a few days." She looked away and changed the subject. "So, where are the kids?"

"Anastasia is at the park; Gabi went out with his friends and Samuele is at work." He noticed that she turned and was heading for the stairs.

"Guliana, where are you going? Don't you want your coffee?" He quickly asked her.

"Yes, I do. I'm just going to pat these eyes with some cold water. I'll be down in a few minutes, okay?" She answered as she climbed the stairs.

"Okay, I'll start making it then." He yelled back at her.

Giuliana ran into her bathroom and locked the door. She let out all the tears she was withholding before. She tried not to be too loud otherwise her kids would hear, and she didn't want that. She washed her face with cold water. She realized that she had to suffer in silence, but it was so hard to keep this to herself. Happiness was much easier to hide than sadness. "I've got to tell someone!" She whispered as she shed more tears.

She thought of Bobby. Bobby was one of her chat buddies. He was a very dear man, and he knew all about Aaron. Bobby was a Firefighter and he lived in California. He was also a bit jealous of Aaron because he loved Giuliana too. He would have wanted to have a relationship with her, but he was too far away. Giuliana knew about his feelings for her, but she just considered him as a dear friend. She decided she was going online tonight and confessing everything to Bobby. She was sure that he would have been a great shoulder to cry on.

She came downstairs and began dinner. She was happy that she was by herself as she prepared dinner because she was able to hide her tears from the rest of the family. After dinner she went for her usual walk. As she walked, she thought of the events of the day and her tears deluged.

When Giuliana came home, she dried her eyes again and once again she put on a happy face and turned on her computer. She waited patiently for it to turn on and for the chat line to turn on. It was only ten minutes after ten and Bobby wouldn't have been on until eleven at least. She navigated the net until she saw that Bobby had come online.

Hi, Bobby, are you there?

After a few minutes she noticed his status changed to "online".

Yes, Giuliana, I am.

Oh Bobby! I feel awful!

She went for the tissues again.

What's wrong?

He didn't like the sound of that.

It's over, Bobby, over…and I'm a wreck!

She could still remember the words written in the emails.

Tell me, Giuliana, I'm here for you.

What did he do to her?

It was so bad. He finished it today through emails, and I'm a mess!

She was weeping again.

> *I can't believe it! Through email, couldn't he have told you in person?'*

This man had no backbone!

I guess not! God! I can't take this…it hurts so much!

She laid her head on the desk.

> *Son of a bitch! He's lucky I live in California!*

He was fuming!

Yes, he is. You know, Bobby, I felt it on Friday. I don't know…he was just different…

She still felt her stomach turn.

> *Why, did you meet on Friday?*

Yes. Not for long though and it was also kind of funny…

> *Funny? How?*

Well, between the kissing and the rest…he kept talking about his family situation and how busy he is at work. He doesn't usually talk about his wife, especially when we're together. He's never

shown me a picture of her either. That's why he seemed changed.

She certainly guessed it.

> *And you felt it? That's called women's*
>
> *intuition, isn't it?*

He was well aware of the power of a woman's intuition.

Oh, yes. Mine is very well developed. Even today, as he replied to

my initial emails, I felt that something was wrong and then he

dropped the bomb!

And what a bomb!

> *Giuliana, this guy is a player and a*
>
> *big liar. You gave him what he wanted*
>
> *and now he's dumped you. I wish I*
>
> *were there to hold you and help you*
>
> *through this! Damn!*

He also wanted to kick the shit out of him!

No, Bobby, he's not a player, I was his only one [besides his

wife], I'm sure of that. I know he's not a liar either, he just didn't

tell me everything so I wouldn't be hurt.

Her love for him was his defense.

*But you ARE hurt! What really
bothers me is that he broke it to you in
an email and at work even! If he was
a real man, he would have told you in
person!*

She was so in love that she didn't see this.

*Yes, you're right there. He should have told me in person, and I
did say that to him in one of my replies. I wish you were here too
because I have nobody here, I can tell. My hubby is out of the
question, my sister has her own problems, and my mother...no
way! My best friend wouldn't understand how I got myself in this
situation because she doesn't like my chatting. So, you're all I
have left, Bobby.*

She was really leaning on him right now.

*I'm glad I am. You've got to be strong
and make sure nobody notices
anything because you could lose your
family because of this. Now, you've got*

to get on with your life like nothing ever happened. You'll be in my thoughts, and I'll pray for you, Giuliana and promise me you'll pray too.

God was her only strength and prayer was her connection with him.

Oh yes, I will. I'm sure that God will help me through this. I've been through a lot of rough times in my life, and I know I'm strong, I'll get over him, sooner or later.

She was certain of that.

That's the spirit! You'll make it, you'll see. If you need to, just call mA, anytime, day or night. I'll be here to comfort you, even if it's just through chat or by phone. Okay?

He knew Giuliana well enough to know that she could get through this.

Thanks, Bobby. I really appreciate this, and I'll make it up to you some day, I promise. You're a real friend.

She had become very attached to Bobby.

I wish I were more than a friend for

you, Giuliana, I would never hurt you.

You know how I feel about you. Come

to California! Say you need a vacation

and come here for a few days; you can

stay with me. I'll help you forget him,

trust me!

God! He wanted to hold her tight and make her forget all her problems.

Oh, Bobby! You know I can't. I've just started my job and I

don't have any vacation. What would I tell my hubby? I've never

gone on vacation without him. I know how you feel about mA,

and I've always told you that I do love you but as a dear friend

you know that it can't go any further. Especially now. I'm sorry

Bobby. I know that you would heal all my wounds, but you'll

have to do it through the chat line. Is that okay?

She had to clear things up between them.

Okay, agreed. But could you at least call me?

My cell number is 310-395-4681. Please, let

me help you, Giuliana.

He wasn't happy about that, but it didn't mean that he would give up on her.

Ok, I saved it. I'll call you tomorrow night while I go for my walk

or tell me what time is best for you?

She wrote his number on a sticky note and hid it in a compartment in her wallet.

I'm off tomorrow and for a couple of

days after that. Call me anytime, I'll

keep my cell on and charged.

He preferred the telephone and he really wanted to hear her voice.

Ok, Bobby, I will call you. I have to thank you; you're helping me

so much already. I really do feel better.

She did feel a bit relieved now.

I feel better too. You're a great gal,

Giuliana, and you don't deserve this.

Although, I've got to tell you that you went looking for it. The very moment you agreed to meet him. I did warn you about him, remember?

He had to remind her that he was always acting in her best interest.

Yes, I remember, and I should have listened to you and now I'm paying for it! I shouldn't have fallen in love with him so easily and now it hurts so much!

Her eyes were filling with tears again.

You can't command love or control it. When you fall, you fall. That's the way love is.

Just like he was not in control when he fell for Giuliana.

Yes, I know. I really did it, didn't I? I could kick myself for getting into this mess!

Once again, she dried her eyes.

Giuliana don't do this to yourself, please! It happened and now you just

*have to deal with it…you're strong
and you can do it! I have faith in you
and God will help you too, trust him!*

His faith was very deep.

*Thanks, Bobby, your words are like a warm blanket. I know I
can make it with your support.*

Even through the computer screen she felt his warmth.

*You're welcome. I'll always be here for
you, Giuliana, no matter what.*

*I know. Well, I'd should try and get some sleep, I've got work
tomorrow. Night Bobby, and thanks.*

*Night, Giuliana, I wish I could hold
you all night in my arms…*

This was also one of his recurring dreams.

*I would really like that tonight…I know you would make me
forget all my troubles, but I can dream of it and I will.*

*So will I. Good Night, Giuliana…I
love you.*

Night…me too.

Giuliana turned off the computer and whipped her eyes. She felt better and worse at the same time. She was happy that she was able to cry on Bobby's should but at the same time she was lonely, and she didn't want to be lonely tonight.

She went to bed and quietly wept to sleep.

As soon as she woke up, she was already thinking of Aaron. She couldn't forget him so easily; he had been her first thought in the morning and her last thought at night for the past three months. She went to the bathroom and looked in the mirror.

"I look horrible! Stop crying Giuliana!" She yelled at her image, but her eyes were already filled with tears that couldn't be stopped. She didn't bother putting make up because it would have been whipped off in no time. She remembered the tie she bought for Aaron and went looking for it. It was nicely tucked away in her underwear drawer. She left it there and went to work. She was thinking of writing him a letter and mailing it to him along with the tie.

When she arrived at work she followed the daily ritual,

coffee, turned on the computer, take all messages and reply to all emails. It saddened her not to find an email from Aaron, enough to make her eyes water again. She opened up the email from the day before and read it again. As she read it, she still couldn't believe it. It was over, really over. She was crying again. She went to the bathroom to wash her face. When she came out she bumped into her boss.

"Hi Giuliana. My God! Are you okay?" She was looking at her face.

"No, not good at all." she answered as her eyes filled with tears again.

Karen began rubbing her shoulders and asked, "Is there something wrong here at work?"

Giuliana tried to answer "Oh, No! Work is great. It's something else and it's private so I really......can't say."

"Oh, okay. You don't have to tell me anything, don't worry. Do you want to go home? I'll have someone cover for you today." Karen asked with sincere worry.

"No, I'm fine. I need to stay at work, it keeps my mind

occupied." She answered as she reached her desk and pulled up a tissue. "I'll be fine, it'll just take some time that's all."

"Okay, Giuliana. But if you change your mind, just let me know." She said as she patted Giuliana's hand.

"I will." She really liked Karen. She was nice to her right from the start, and she made Giuliana feel at ease in the workplace. She was quite happy with her job all in all.

Her morning dragged on as usual. Although being very miserable, she was still trying to make a good impression. When lunch time came, she started on her letter. She wrote many drafts before she decided on her final version.

Dearest Aaron,

This is the little something I bought you. Naturally, I can't keep it. I couldn't bear to see it on my husband or my sons. It was bought with you in mind and the color, red, representing love and passion…exactly what we could have had. I honestly don't care what you do with it; wear it (so you'll have a little reminder of mA, if you do), throw it away or give it away.

I really had a horrible day yesterday! You sure dropped a hell of a bomb! I was crying continuously, I couldn't work, I couldn't eat a bite and what I did eat, I threw up, I was nauseous and lightheaded. I'm hoping you're suffering as much as mA, but I doubt it. My husband noticed my eyes, when I got home, and asked me if I was crying. I told him it was some sort of eye infection and he fell for it.

I did tell my closest and dearest chat buddy, Bobby, remember I told you about him. I had to tell somebody! I'm good at hiding happiness but not suffering. I told him everything, right from that very first night on chat. So, he'll be my shoulder to cry on for a while.

Mind you, I will get over you, Aaron, it may take a week, a month or more, I don't know, but I will succeed.

Finally, I want to thank you, for making me feel young again, for giving me love and a little bit of romance that I need so much, for your wonderful thoughts that I will treasure forever and for being strong for the both of us, thanks.

Well, this is it! I had to write you this letter to officially break it. You won't hear from me again, I promise! Although, right now, it's so hard for me to keep this promise.

Aaron, let me close by giving you a bit of hope. If you ever have a change of heart, or if your wife leaves you or if you free yourself of the situation, you're in now, please call me. I promise I will not ruin your life or mine. I'll be happy with the little time we can spend together.

I will always love you, Aaron,

Giuliana

By the time Giuliana re-read the letter she was crying again. She folded it and put it into her purse. Once again, she went to the bathroom to wash her face and dry her eyes.

When Giuliana got home, she took the tie from its hiding place and went to the mall. She went to the post office, bought a medium-sized envelope, placed the tie and the letter inside, wrote his business address and mailed it.

Her eyes were filling with tears as the clerk weighed it and sent it off. As she placed it in the bin, Giuliana turned around and pulled out a tissue.

"Goodbye Aaron." She whispered as she left the office.

She thought she'd better do some browsing as she told her family that she was going shopping even though she was definitely not in the mood for shopping.

TO BE CONTINUED...

I truly hope you enjoyed this first part of this trilogy titled "With All of Me"…

As an indie…

…(independent) author, I rely on reviews. In fact, those gold stars are the indie authors' lifelines. If you truly care about your favorite indie author, or any other indie, please leave a review on at least one of the following websites:

Amazon - www.Amazon.com

Barnes & Noble - www.barnesandNoble.com

BookBub- www.Bookbub.com

Goodreads - www.Goodreads.com

Google Books - https://play.google.com

iBooks App - https://iBooks.com

Thank you so much for your support. Please, don't ever forget—I write for you!

All the best from your favorite author,

Joanne Fisher

ABOUT THE AUTHOR

Greetings,

I'm Joanne Fisher. A Canadian-Italian-American author and I have penned 17 books so far. I dabble in several genres: steamy romances, historical fictions, murder/mysteries. I also write Christmas novellas giving them an Italian flair with delectable recipes at the back. Because of my love for travel, I have also penned 3 non-fiction travel guides titled "Traveling Boomers" I also love writing short stories and I've collected 13 in "Baker's Dozen Anthology", all about love! I have written many short stories for SCWG anthologies of which I am currently very active. I live in Central Florida with hubby, and our beloved Doxie, Wally.

I encourage you to visit my website at

www.JoannesBooks.com